THE CRONES' TALES

BY ALYCE ELMORE

FAIRYTALES

FOR

FEMINISTS

First published in 2026 by

© Alyce Elmore 2026

National Library of Australia Cataloguing-in-Publication entry:

118404

ISBN 97817638502-3-1 (Paperback)

ISBN 97817638502-4-8 (E-Book 3.0)

Printed in Australia by Ingram Spark

Cover Design by Alyce Elmore

Formatted using Lacuna

Also By

Alyce Elmore

Novels

When All Hope Is Lost

Pray to the Dead

For Where There Are Harps

Audio Dramas

https://fancifulflights.bandcamp.com/

Tales From The Future

Tales Beyond Belief

Follow Alyce Elmore on

Substack https://alyceelmore.substack.com

And on her website www.alyceelmore.com

Facebook https://www.facebook.com/alyce.elmoreauthor

About The Author

JUST WHO DO YOU THINK YOU ARE?

Alyce Elmore got tired of being asked that question, deciding instead to write about it. Her short stories and novels search for answers by scavenging through time and place, exploring the real and the fantastic and along the way encountering the outrageous and the mundane. She has lived in major cities around the world, journeyed through jungles, hiked in the mountains and currently resides in an off grid shed in the middle of nowhere. To date, she has no answers, just lots of clues but she invites her readers to hitch a ride anyway because a search for the unknowable is in itself an enjoyable quest.

To those who have worked to ensure that everyone has a chance at equality

Foreword

Please join us for a night of scintillating conversations, engaging modern day versions of well-known fairy tales and a tankard of mulled wine. That's the invitation The Crones' Tales extends to you. Five women, each representative of her era in the women's movement towards equality, meet and share history, the etymology of words used to label women, and of course, their tales. You may recognise Mary Wollstonecraft in the character of Beatrice for she was unique, a lone woman's voice lost in the louder male voices of the Age of Enlightenment. One that would remain silent for almost a century after her death. Margret, however, is part of a movement. She is decidedly an American suffragist who resents the diminutive use of the term suffragette but regardless of nationality she speaks for all the women who felt the time had come for them to have a say in government. Ginger comes from my mother's generation and tries to explain why they retreated to the suburbs to give birth to the 70s' feminists. Those second wave feminists, along with their seeming contradictions, are encapsulated in the character of Verna. Her daughter Chloe, is absent. The generation following the baby boomers is left to deal with both the advances made by their mothers and the backlash created by women obtaining more independence. And then, there is Florence, the youngest and most inclusive of them all. Her voice extends beyond that of women. She wants equality for all of humanity as well as the Earth and its other creatures. The intent of this book is to show that feminism, like any great movement, is made up of many voices and as the women in this evening of camaraderie point out, they will not be silenced, not even by each other.

Table Of Contents

Chapter 1

CHANGE WAS IN THE AIR

W IND PUMMELED BEATRICE'S FRAIL BODY AS SHE LEFT HER
house. It stole her breath, and the sharpness of its chill sliced at her
skin. How the day had changed! The morning had held such promise, and
she'd been excited by the prospect of seeing her sisters, Margret, Ginger,
Verna, Chloe and Florence for an evening of camaraderie and story telling.
Then at midday, there had been a sudden shift. The temperature had
dropped, the wind had increased and the sun had taken shelter behind the
clouds. As the afternoon progressed, those clouds grew darker, angrier.
But Beatrice wasn't about to let a little bad weather stand in the way of
tonight's meeting of the sisterhood. Their meetings, few and far between,
were far too important, so she packed away her light summer shawl, pulled
out her heavy winter cloak and thus armed to face the storm, left the
warmth and comfort of her house.

For the weather to turn suddenly on a warm autumn day was not unusual, but there was something in this wind that portended more than a

shift in the weather. there was something she could feel, but couldn't put her finger on. Vague and grey as a dream, it loomed on the rim of her consciousness, veiled and unwilling to show itself. It worried her; not so much for herself, but for the others. She'd had her day and brief as it was, had left her mark. But the other sisters, for all that they had made greater strides than she, still relied on her for guidance, especially when times were uncertain. And today certainly had become uncertain. On the other hand, she reminded herself as she closed the gate and headed out onto the road, uncertainty wasn't always a bad thing. It often led to change and change, for better or worse, was necessary.

Now that she was underway, with her destination clear, she took a deep calming breath. Change was definitely in the air. It was carried on the wind that had earlier blown, first one way, then another; in the way the warm glow of summer had given way to the fading red of autumn and now in the lengthening shadows that Beatrice feared were intent on concealing and misleading her. The signs that change was coming were everywhere, and yet, Beatrice couldn't intuit their meaning. That, in itself, was not surprising. Change was unpredictable. Those who suggested they could predict it, often claimed the ability after the fact. And yet, there were some, who sensing that the time was right, knew how to take control. They were the ones who used change as a sail to propel themselves to the front.

The winds, that had started as nothing more than a nuisance pushed harder against her. Picking up, gusts created isolated whirligigs that blew in a confused and disorganized fashion that ripped decisively at all that defied them. They sent unsecured items, paper, garbage bins, and children's things scurrying. They tore leaves from the trees. They broke branches and toppled those that wouldn't bend. But in the midst of the chaos, Beatrice began to detect method in the seemingly random wind. The more she observed, the more she read meaning in the way the wind stripped away both the leaves that were fading and ready to go as well as the green who would have held on a bit longer. It was a pattern she had employed herself.

On her own tree of life, she'd plucked some leaves while encouraging others. She'd removed from her life's tree, a father who could have shared his wealth evenly between his children but instead left all to his only son. She'd pruned from her life the brother who doled out a pittance of his inheritance to his sisters, for it was only meant to be a dowry to convince some other man to take responsibility for them. But there were leaves she would have kept. The green and vibrant leaf of a dashing young man who promised marriage and then disappeared in the first gentle breeze. The sister who grew on the same branch but was plucked by a passing stranger and placed in a vase. Once her beauty faded, she'd been tossed out and forgotten. And then there were the leaves that, despite losing color with the passage of time, refused to drop. They were the ones who'd believed in her, encouraged her, supported her and now were remembered because of her. Thus, she had changed and shaped her tree of life, but what lives would this wind change? How would it prune and shape, not only the solid oaks but the saplings that were still so young and impressionable?

Wearied by her struggles, she turned down a dark and narrow laneway that connected one street with the next. Although foreboding, it offered her reprieve from the wind. In the lane it was quiet, but the shadows were deeper. Overhead the clouds scurried as if late for an appointment and within the houses, lights came on. She had the sense that time was running out, as if it were something that existed in some pre-measured quantity. With renewed purpose, she rushed past one house after the other until she reached the street's end. Rounding the corner, she was once again caught up in the full force of the changing weather. A reminder that the laneway had been only a temporary shelter from the growing storm.

Finding her once again, the wind renewed its assault. in response, she lowered her head and continued against it. In retaliation, it grabbed her cloak, urging it to come and dance - if she would not. Defiantly, she drew her cloak tighter, fearing its own willfulness. In her youth, she too had been headstrong and like the cloak that now threatened to abandon her, she would have frolicked with the wild wind. She'd have coyly turned her back to it and allowed it to push her along. She'd have turned and followed its whims as if they were her own, conversing with it in a language only lovers understood, seducing and being seduced. In those heady days, change had been as irresistible as a siren's call. But change was a wild creature that refused domestication. The promise of something new and beautiful that turned into something monstrous, a hideous, destructive thing. What appeared as delightful as the adorable and ever-changing chameleon, grew up to be a dragon; a creature you either mounted and took charge of, or let it devour you. So many of her sisters hadn't understood that. They'd been so eager to embrace change that they'd fallen prey to it. And those who never saw it coming, who failed to read the signs, got caught in the turbulence of its wake. No matter how you desired, ignored or rejected change, it transformed you, and now Beatrice felt its coming once again. Only now, she felt how dangerous it was to be all alone.

Like the houses, clustered together for protection and companionship, she craved the company of her sisters but the safety of the village gave way to open fields. Here the wind had free rein as there was no longer anything to stand in its way. It flattened the tall grass. Stripped blossoms from the flowers that lined the road and scattered the summer's seed. Overhead, a flash of light illuminated vague shapes. What was this thing riding on the wind? In a moment of clarity, she realized that there was only one way to find out. Instead of cowering before it, she had to expose herself to it. Face it full on. Opening her cloak, she felt it billow out. The storm's full fury attacked her. Holding her in its embrace, it fingered the white strands of her hair, and memories of other hands flooded back. Long-silenced passions pulsed through her veins as she willed herself to read what was in the air. Was this storm the harbinger of an ending or the beginning of a new age? Either was likely to be destructive so should she warn her sisters to stay still, take solace in what was, dream of what could be, or was this a time to grab on and ride the beast? The wind pulled harder, yanking her hair, pulling the breath from her lungs. Her fingers tightened on her cloak as the wind tried to strip it from her, but instead of feeling its soft, reassuring cloth, she felt something cold and unyielding. Electricity shot up her arm, but still she hung on. A moment longer and she might know for sure if this storm was blowing away the dead and dying to create something new and beautiful or if it was only bringing destruction.

Suddenly the roar of the wind gave way to the sounds of laughter. The change startled her, breaking the spell. She looked down to see her hand, not grasping her cloak, but holding onto a gate. What shook her, however, was her hand. She stared in horror. Her fingers, like summer's roots left in the ground over winter, had become gnarled dry things. While they were attached to her, she no longer recognized them as her own. Was she shriveling up? Disappearing? Was that what the storm was trying to tell her? That her time was over, or worse yet, that the sisterhood itself was dying?

Not yet, she whispered. *Not yet.*

With shaking hands, she lifted the latch and entered the front yard. Through the window of the small cottage, bounded by the white picket fence, came the welcome sight of a glowing fire. Shadows moved inside, but they were welcome shadows and the sound that floated out was that of cheery voices. This was her destination, the house of the youngest of their sisterhood, Florence. Here was her true and lasting sanctuary. Like the bud that swells on the branch, the girl was their yet to be fulfilled promise, their hope for the future, the sum of all their voices. This was their response to the storm.

In the distance, thunder rumbled and Beatrice looked defiantly at the sky. *You can do your best to drown me out, but I will not be silenced.* Standing before the door, she raised her hand to knock, but the wind countered with a renewed attack. It grabbed savagely at her cloak. She clung onto it with one hand and raised the other to bang on the door but another flash of light stayed her hand, She turned, sensing something coming up behind her. Despite the fading light and lengthening shadows, it wasn't totally dark. Still, she couldn't see what was out there. Perhaps, she was wrong. Maybe there was nothing to see, or maybe it just wasn't ready to show itself. She shuddered, more to shake off the feeling of dread than because of the cold.

Once again laughter spilled out from within, a reminder that inside she had companions. Turning her back on the dark and whatever it concealed, she banged firmly on the door. Tonight, perhaps she would share her concerns, but for now, the warmth of companionship beckoned. Tonight, she and her sisters would gather around a warm fire. They would drink hot mulled wine, share a meal and entertain each other with tales both old and new. The evening's theme, fairy tales, had been her choice. For, like the movement itself, fairy tales were handed down from one generation to the next, each interpreting and reinterpreting them in their own way.

As the door swung open, another gust of wind threatened to pull her back into the growing darkness. This time it was stronger, more insistent but it couldn't compete with the hand that grabbed onto her.

Chapter 2

BEATRICE

"At last, you're here," said Florence. "Come in. Come in before this wind carries you away."

Greeted with enthusiasm by the women within, Beatrice felt her spirits lift. It had been some time since they'd last gathered, so once Flo had removed the heavy cloak from her shoulders, the others surrounded her and there was much hugging, laughter, and remarks on the unseasonably cold night. Then, Beatrice smelled the spicy fruitiness of mulled wine as a warm tankard appeared in her hand.

"I haven't held one of these in many a year," she said to Flo. "It takes me back to a time when I was more your age. Where did you find such a thing?"

"On the internet," said their hostess, "you are familiar—" Her voice hesitated.

"I may be out of time but I'm not out of touch. I daresay I know more about your generation than many of your generation know of me. Still, it's nice to have something familiar in my hands again."

"They're not originals," said Flo, "but I thought they would suit tonight's theme better than my modern coffee mugs."

"And perfect they are," replied Beatrice. As she spoke, she again noticed her fingers, the translucence of her skin, the way the knuckles bulged out but she also noticed the hint of colour, especially around her nails, a vague pinkness - a trick of the light or had the warmth of the tankard returned some life to her hands?

"Unlike the weather," said a familiar voice. Beatrice looked up and saw Ginger's smiling face as, tankard in hand, she squeezed past Flo who was hanging Beatrice's cloak in the hall closet. The middle-aged woman with hints of grey in her curly red hair, stopped to add, "Mind you, it's been a long time since we've seen a summer cut this short. Normally, I'd still be sporting shorts and a midriff at this time of year, but instead I had to pull out my turtleneck and trench coat."

Beatrice watched her walk away as Margret came up beside her. They clinked tankards as they both stared longingly at Ginger's bibbed and purple and yellow checked overalls.

"Why didn't we have enough common sense to wear trousers?" said Beatrice.

"Perhaps because of what they did to women who dared to do so. *Les citoyennes* who dared to think that liberty, equality and fraternity included them."

"The *sans-culottes*," said Beatrice, "they overthrew one men's club only to install another. Where's the progress in that?"

"Women were welcomed when they were needed and told to put their skirts back on once the new men were put in charge," replied Margret.

"Your revolution wasn't much better," added Beatrice.

"Maybe so, but it gave us a framework on which to pin our hopes."

"Or cage you in," replied Beatrice. "Laws, like clothes, can hide a multitude of sins." Then stepping back, she looked Margret up and down. "You've worn the blue sash today."

Like Beatrice, Margret's clothing exemplified the modesty of a middle-class women of her era. More restrained than Beatrice, who'd been quite radical for her time, neither pushed the boundaries of dress beyond acceptable levels of decency, which meant that although separated by more than a century, for that is how long it took for Beatrice's ideas to filter out to other women, they both wore skirts that touched the floor. The primary difference in their dress, aside from Margret's sash, was in their silhouettes. Not the actual shape of their bodies, for women have always come in all shapes and sizes, but in the dictates imposed by fashion. For fashion, above all else, dictated how a women's body should look, and clothing functioned to mold women's individuality into the prevailing archetype. Beatrice, a product of the Age of Enlightenment, wore a neoclassical dress reminiscent of the post-revolution period. One that neither distorted nor hid the female form. It was a time when stays were required to support the bust, and much as Beatrice hated them, she felt naked without their presence. Margret, on the other hand, sported a dress that expanded her bust with frills and balloon sleeves, while using corsets to shrink the waist but Beatrice noted that tonight Margret had foregone the bustle, that ridiculous protrusion meant to draw the eye to a woman's rear. Where one period hid feminine curves, the other emphasised them, and Beatrice couldn't help but think that the first feminists, despite rallying for women's rights, were careful not to look too mannish in the process. That was the mistake her French counterparts had made.

Beatrice sighed, "I longed to wear those red and white *pantalons* and the *carmagnole* of the women in Paris."

"If you had, you might have wound up in jail," said Margret.

"Or decapitated like poor Olympe." The voice belonged to Verna. Standing behind the two elders, she towered over them, not only because she was taller but because she wore shoes, that Beatrice thought defied both gravity and common sense. With those long thin heels, Verna appeared to be walking on daggers.

"Murdered for writing the Declaration of the Rights of Women," Verna stated. "Well, I suppose women have been murdered for less." Then, shoulders back, body erect, the woman of indeterminate age walked past. With deliberate, well-placed steps and hips swaying ever so seductively, she catwalked her way towards the other room, while over her shoulder, she said, "Coming?"

Beatrice, both awed and astounded by Verna's skill, couldn't speak. It was like watching a high-wire act. With every step, she expected Verna to slip and topple and so she held her breath, ready to gasp if her sister should falter, while at the same time, willing her on until, at last Verna disappeared into the other room. As unexpected as the performance had been, in its own way, it was uniquely Verna. Like so many of her personas, she'd mastered this one as well. But that wasn't surprising. Of all of them, Verna had seen, and often instigated, the most dramatic changes. Ginger may have witnessed a time when both women's hair and skirts were chopped short; when wars spanned continents instead of mere countries and when women both advanced and retreated; but Verna had seen women stand up and demand to be heard. Women of the latter part of the 20th century, didn't ask for their rights, they demanded them and, in the process, created a movement that saw women escape the bonds of wifedom and emerge victorious in the workplace. In a single generation, women expanded the professions they were permitted to pursue. They moved beyond teaching the lower grades to taking positions as professors and deans. No longer restrained to being nurses, they became doctors. They began by petitioning for more rights and wound up becoming lawyers, judges and law makers. They calculated the numbers that would take men into space and invented machines. And with their goal within their sights, they stalled. The juggernaut came to a standstill. And it wasn't men who stopped them, although the barriers they built were impressive, it was women and their own infighting. For all that Verna had accomplished, the freedom to have a career, to buy a house in her own name, to travel where she liked and on her own, to make love to whoever she liked and to decide if and when to have children - for all that - Beatrice felt something was not quite right. Perhaps Verna's push to succeed in a man's world had made her question her own femininity. That would explain the way she dressed, this evening.

Tonight, despite the cold, Verna wore a short tight skirt, one that rose well above her knees, and a tight sweater that did little to contain the movement of her voluptuous breasts. What began with discarding restrictive undergarments became a proclamation that a woman's body was her own. Was that obscene? Exhibitionist? Too provocative? Or had Verna embraced her divine feminine. Regardless of the statement made by her clothing, Beatrice had to admit, Verna had done more to give women freedom than any other generation. Which meant that she was always going to be a hard act to follow.

"And this is what we fought and died to achieve," said Margret, expressing her own thoughts on Verna's outfit.

"I don't know," said Beatrice. "I think she makes me feel old and out of date, like an anachronism."

"That's because she thinks she invented feminism."

Which was an interesting comment from the woman who claimed title to the first wave of feminism, as if, throughout history, there had been no other push for women's rights. Well, perhaps they hadn't been organised into a movement. They were lone voices asking why they were denied education, professions, independence. Out loud she said, "Feminism comes in all shapes and sizes." Then, looking around, she added, "Speaking of which, isn't someone missing?"

"You don't know?" Margret leaned close. "Chloe's husband has gone too far this time."

"How serious is it?"

Margret shrugged her shoulders and shook her head. "She," pointing discreetly at Verna, "won't talk to me about it, but I know it's serious."

Beatrice looked in Verna's direction. "Poor Verna. I suppose she thinks she's to blame."

"For every bit of ground we gain, some men will feel it's there's we've taken," replied Margret.

"Ladies," said Flo, grabbing Beatrice in one arm and Margret with the other, "We're moving to the living room where I think you'll find the fire and the seating more conducive to stories of dark woods, magical creatures and princesses than this entryway."

Beatrice had never been to Flo's house before, and as they entered what Flo called her living room, she saw a room that embraced life. Plants filled the room. They lined up in front of the large window that looked out over the garden beds and onto the orchard beyond where the garden ran up against the wild wood. Unlike the front yard, the garden lacked any fencing, just open space that suggested boundless possibilities. Whereas the rooms of Beatrice's time had been small, with low ceilings and tiny windows that barely let in the light, this room opened itself to the world, and Beatrice felt both proud and envious. Proud that women had made such progress and envious because she hadn't had the opportunity herself.

The men of the Enlightenment had installed their own grand windows that opened them up to new ideas. Called coffee shops, they percolated, not only with the novel brew, but with discussions on scientific papers, debates on political systems, and critiques of the latest novels. Those coffee shops exemplified the Age of Enlightenment, but how enlightened was a society that only listened to a small minority; one that was predominantly male, mostly white, and invariably European? What had those men accomplished that she couldn't achieve, given the same chance? Even now, all these years later, she felt the sting of being excluded from the opportunities they took for granted. The opportunity to study, to attend university, to earn a decent wage. The men of her day wrote grandly of universal rights for all, but when her essay laid out logically, rationally and unequivocally why women were every bit as intelligent as men, her critics discarded it as a frilly bit of woman's dribble. And those critics weren't exclusively male. In fact, the small circle of supporters, the ones who praised her work, were male. The women she expected to support her, turned their back on her, preferring to remain in the safety of acceptable women's literature – romance novels and children's books. In the end, it didn't matter. Her work was dismissed and nearly forgotten. The voices against equality for women were too loud.

We will not be silenced.

Someone said - that even when they severed Olympe's head from her body - she spoke those words. True or not. Those words now belonged to the sisterhood. They were women from different eras who didn't always agree, but listened anyway, for they all knew what it was like to be shouted down. To be silenced. But in this room, there was no silence. All around her, Beatrice heard the voices of her sisters talking with each other, laughing. It was a good sound.

Flo appeared by her side and, taking her arm, guided her towards her seat. While Beatrice had allowed her thoughts to wander, the others had organised the chairs in a semi-circle before the fire. The seat of honour, the one near the fire facing the large window, they reserved for Beatrice.

One by one, they took their seats; Margret next to Beatrice, Ginger, next in age, took the next seat, followed by Verna and finally, their hostess, Flo, who took the seat opposite Beatrice. Between them, they would keep the fire going, for it was going to be a long night.

"Tonight, as you set the theme, it is your duty to begin," said Flo.

Beatrice, nestled in her chair, took a long sip of her mulled wine. Already she felt younger, stronger, more alive, as the dread she'd felt earlier withdrew to a dark corner of the room. There might be more life in her yet, she thought. So, as the wind howled around the tiny cottage, and the women moved their chairs closer to each other, Beatrice set aside her drink and prepared to tell her tale.

"You may have heard this story before, for it has been told and retold many times, and in those tellings, the woman at the centre of it is portrayed as the hapless maid caught up in the intrigues of powerful men.

The main protagonists, the boastful male, the greedy king and the grasping troll, all play their part to prove to this maid that she is subservient in every way. But the real story is in how she outsmarted every one of them and in doing so, freed herself."

"It's a good start," said Margret, pulling out her knitting and settling back in her own chair as Beatrice began the tale.

Chapter 3

WHAT'S IN A NAME?

MY FATHER WAS A BOASTER. A MAN SO REMOVED FROM REALITY, not by drink or idiocy, but by his own arrogance, that he couldn't help but assert his own self-importance. This need was so great that no claim was too ridiculous, no lie too outrageous, and no pig-ignorant jest too preposterous for him to tell. There were those who laughed and called him a buffoon, but when hard times came, even buffoons can have an audience – if – they make the promises everyone wants to hear. Now, it's one thing when the men who gather in the pub, nod and aye a man with more bravado than bravery, especially when he buys a round, but it's quite another thing, when the king invites him to court and takes his boasts seriously. Which is where I come in.

My story revolves around a name. And you might be asking yourself at this point, "What's in a name?"

As it turns out, everything and nothing.

My story begins before I became Queen, but I'll start there because it's where I learned that men's names mean much but not so women's. When I asked the most learned man in the kingdom, the priest, why this should be so, he said that God had given Adam the right to name every animal so that he could have dominion over them. Presumably, this meant that Adam named Eve as well, for otherwise, why would every man believe that they should have dominion over every woman? But that was when I believed in the power of names. In those days, I believed that someone called King knew how to rule. I believed that someone called father would provide and protect. I even believed that if straw were spun into gold, then it had more value than my own precious possessions. What I learned, however, is that names have no more power than what we give them.

Now, I'm sure you already know this story as surely as you know the scoundrel's name but at the time, I knew neither, just as I suspect you know little or nothing of who I am or how I felt about the whole situation. For just as I was kept ignorant of my father's boasting and my King's greed, you have been kept ignorant of its main character. Me. So, let me start by saying that everyone in this story had a choice, including me. The difference was that I bore the consequences of my decisions, which is why I learned an important lesson, while they did not.

But I digress. The lesson, or as you would say, the moral of the story, must wait.

First, I will give you an example of how men use power to their advantage. Once I became Queen, I sat by my husband's side and observed how he dealt with his subjects. It happened one day that a moneylender came demanding payment.

The King listened to the man's demands then said haughtily, "I'll pay what I borrowed but not a penny more."

"But the interest, m'lord," said the man.

Slamming his sceptre hard on the floor, the King shouted, "Interest be damned. Charging interest is illegal. I can have you jailed for that."

"But we agreed—".

"A contract made under duress is not a legally binding one. Now, if I were you, I'd take my offer before I throw you in jail."

When this gnarled little man appeared before me, demanding his due, I remembered how the King had treated the moneylender and thought to use my title as Queen, in the same way. Alas, we women have much to learn about how power works. When I repeated those same words, mentioning contracts made under duress and interest being illegal, the horrid creature laughed in my face.

"If anyone has done something illegal, it's you. You deceived the King into marrying you by claiming you'd turned straw into gold. Then, you promised away your firstborn, something over which you have no ownership, for the law stipulates that the firstborn belongs to the King, not the Queen. The way I see it, and the way I think the courts will see it, it's you that's broken the law."

What did I, a mere peasant girl with no learning, know of the law? Nothing. Absolutely nothing. What I did understand, however, was that kings could create or change laws to suit their own needs. And why was this so? Because men had granted such power to kings, but not to queens. What worked for the King didn't work for me as Queen, not because one argument was more ethically sound than the other, but because the King had power over not just men, but the law, whereas I did not.

And so, there I was, facing this horrid little man, who repeated his demand.

"The child is mine."

If power and law were not on my side, I looked for other means and remembered how my King had dealt with a more powerful monarch. When the kingdom was threatened with invasion, instead of fighting, the King sent an envoy offering his opponent a tribute. There was much negotiation, but eventually a price was agreed, and the two men shook hands and signed a treaty. Money was paid and conflict averted. The thought occurred to me that, like the King, perhaps I could buy my way out of my difficulties.

"On the night I made that deal," I said, "I was a simple maid, but now I am a Queen so name your price."

"M'lady," his tone was mocking, "you dare offer money to someone who can spin straw into gold."

He had a point, and I was getting desperate.

Power, the law and now even money had failed me. It was obvious that as a woman, I could not rely on the same ploys that served men. I would have to employ my feminine wiles. Much as I loathed the creature and his hold on me, I fell back on the method women for centuries have employed to great effect.

I fell on my knees and begged.

"I pray, sir, do not hold me to that promise."

The tears I shed were real, but the imp only laughed as men do when a woman prostrates herself before them and instead of showing me some mercy, he reached for the babe in my arms.

"Never," I said as I called for the guards.

You might think that that was what changed his mind. But the truth is, no one came, not even the nursemaid.

No, I was on my own and terrified, just as I had been on the night that I made that promise, and it's only now, as I look back on these events, that I realise how much fear has always influenced my actions. It was fear that kept me silent when my father boasted of my skill. It was fear that kept me silent when the king demanded I spin straw into gold. And it was fear that drove me to bargain away my child. Fear and fear alone had kept me silent when I should have made my voice heard.

I thought of that day when the King first had me brought to the castle.

"Your father says you have a talent for spinning. He says you can spin anything, even turn straw into gold."

I responded in a quavering voice, "M'lord, there's some mistake—"

But the King silenced me with his raised hand. Looking at my father, he said, "If your daughter fails the test, I'm about to give her, she will perish. That is the price of your boasting."

"Father," I cried out, "please plea for my life."

But my father said nothing. He bowed his head as the King laughed and said, "Take heart, Miller. She's only a girl and not your firstborn." Then he ordered me to be taken away.

I remember thinking as they led me away that it was demeaning to be cast aside so lightly. It was true that females were not counted as firstborns but I, as my father's only child, surely counted for something. But my father made no plea, and I was led away to face another, even worse fate, for that was the night I first met my tormentor.

And now that tormentor was standing before me demanding his due, and all I could do was weep and cry as I clutched my newborn to my breast. Then the strangest thing happened. The creature stayed his hand. A look crossed his face. It was a look that chilled me to the bone, for it was the look of someone who knew he'd won but wanted to enjoy the game a bit longer.

He ran a withered finger down my cheek, and in that moment, I froze, fearful of what he might ask this time. For I'd seen that look before. It was on that first night, and it's true that if he'd demanded it, I would have traded my virginity for my life, but that first night, as he reached for me, it was not my body he grabbed but my necklace.

"Give me this token," he said, "and I'll spin this straw into gold."

The necklace was nothing more than bits of knotted string embedded with simple hand-carved beads. Much as I cherished it as a mother's dying gift, I knew it wasn't going to protect me come morning. For when the King found a room of straw and nothing more, he had stipulated that I be put to death. Reluctantly, I removed my mother's gift and immediately felt something important had been lost. It wasn't something I could quantify, but it was a loss, nonetheless. That loss, however, dwindled along with the straw, and hope grew with each strand of gold. My regret at handing over my mother's necklace turned to relief.

In the morning, the beating of my heart muffled the sound of footsteps coming down the hall. As the doors were flung open and the light from the torch brightened the windowless room, I was momentarily blinded until a shadow crossed in front of it. Towering over me was the King himself.

"What have you done with the straw?"

His face was stern. His voice demanding.

"Have you eaten it like some beast of burden?"

"No, M'lord," I stammered. "It's there still but transformed as you requested."

Stepping aside, I pointed at the ground. Strands of gold sat in a neat pile where once there'd been only straw.

Amazed, the King picked them up and handed them to a man standing behind him.

"Is it real, or some ruse sent to make a mockery of me?"

Fear gripped me as I thought I might be felled on the spot, but the man holding the strands said, "It's real, my liege, and of a quality I've never seen before. It is, I believe, pure gold."

The King eyed me as if seeing me for the first time. Of course, he'd seen me the night before when my father brought me to the castle, but then he hadn't really seen me.

"Rather plain for someone who can spin straw into gold."

He laughed. Everyone laughed. Then he signalled for silence and told me my fate.

If only the story had ended with that first night. If only the king had taken the gold that I'd paid for with my mother's love and let me go, then all would have been satisfied. But instead of letting me go, the King said, "Feed her and give her a bed, for I will give her another chance to prove herself."

Why, I wondered, did I have to prove myself again? Wasn't it enough to perform the task once? And now, kneeling before this imp who wanted my child, I felt a rebellion building in my chest. As his gnarled hand stroked my cheek, I saw the same look in his eyes that I had seen in the King's when he sent me a second time into that room.

On that second night too, the imp appeared and once again offered to spin the straw into gold.

"But I have nothing with which to purchase your services."

This time he spotted a simple brass ring on my finger. Touching my hand, I felt a chill as if death's shadow had crossed my path.

"This ring will do."

It had been given me by a lad who blacksmithed next to my father's mill. It was, he said, a token of friendship, but in his eyes, I could see the promise of something more. But what good was a promise if the King found no gold and I lost my head? Sadly, I handed over the ring, and once again the straw was replaced with gold.

Dawn came, and with it the King. This time he shoved me aside and snatched up the golden strands. Relieved, I waited patiently to be released. But it was not release the King had in mind.

"Begin preparations for a banquet, for if this girl spins straw into gold one more time, I shall marry her. If not, we shall feast while she burns."

It was not a proposal. It was a demand. That night I sat before the straw wondering, which was worse, death because I'd failed to do the impossible or life with the King because I had. When the imp appeared a third time, I thought my question answered, for I had nothing left to give. To that dilemma, the imp already had the answer. He pulled back a strand of hair that had fallen over my eyes and said, "I'm willing to wait for my reward. Promise me your firstborn, and I will not only save you but set you up for life."

And so now, here he was, ready to claim what I had agreed to give, and yet his hand stayed. Like the King, I saw in the imp's eyes that he would play this game of his a little longer.

"I'll give you a task. If you complete it, you can keep the child."

What could be worse than losing a child? Eagerly, I replied, "Yes, anything."

"I'll give you three chances to call me by my rightful name."

"Only three," I said.

He made a horrible sound. A giggle, I supposed.

"You're right. There's no fun in that." He rubbed his chin, and a wicked smile spread from ear to ear.

"I'll come every night for three nights and give you three guesses. If by that last guess you fail to call me by my name, I'll have your child."

With that, he was gone, and my baby felt cold against my breast. In a panic, I kissed its lips and hugged it till warmth returned to both of us. That's when I called for the priest and asked my question. He advised me to pray. And so I spent my time in prayer.

I prayed till dawn and through the whole day till at last sleep overtook me and with my babe in my arms my eyes closed. It was in those minutes that precede midnight that my baby stirred and let out a wail. Startled into wakefulness, I found the imp standing next to my bed.

"Have you got a name for me?"

The Bible claimed Jacob to be the father of a nation, so I tried that name first.

The imp shook his head.

Next, I tried Elijah, for he was the prophet on whom the nation waited.

He dismissed that guess with a snort.

For my last guess, I chose Samuel for his wisdom, but alas, it too was wrong.

Leaning in so I could smell his rotten breath, the imp whispered in my ear, "I'm enjoying this game. How about you?"

I cringed, and my baby whimpered as the imp straightened up and vanished. Left alone in the dark, I realised this fiend was a devil and therefore not likely to be found in the good book.

Holding my child close, I whispered, "I will find a way."

The next day, I had my father brought to the castle. I asked him the same question I'd asked the priest.

"Well, a name," he started, then stopped and thought a bit. "A name defines who we are. For example. My name is John, but there are several

Johns in this town, so I'm John Miller, not John Tanner or John Farmer. It's what I do for a living that defines me as a person."

I thought of my mother. Her name was Mary, like many other women in town, and like me she was a spinner, but she wasn't called Mary Spinner. She was called Mary Miller. Her name was defined not by who she was but by who her husband was. So, was the imp defined by what he did or what others thought of him? Either way, I had no idea what the strange little man did for a living besides tricking naïve young women into making promises they didn't want to keep, so I sent my father away and called for the king.

As I waited for him, I reminded myself that this was the man who'd put me in a room three times, each time with the same spinning wheel, and each time with ever more straw and always the same demand. If there was any lesson to be learned, I thought, it was that every time you exceeded someone's expectations they only asked for more.

Still, I was desperate, and so I asked him, "What's in a name?"

He put on a kingly face and said with authority, "I'm referred to by my position in society. They call me King because I am next in line to God. My subjects are named for their positions in relation to mine. The vassals who do my bidding are referred to as Lord so-and-so, while the knights who do the lord's bidding are named Sir So-and-So. And then, of course, there are the serfs. They are called peas-ants because they are as important as a pea and as insignificant as an ant." Then he laughed at his own joke.

Insignificant? The powerful ruled not because of their proximity to God but because they had weapons. And it was the unimportant peasants who kept them fed and clothed while getting nothing in return. As for women, it was much the same. This child at my breast, the king claimed as his own, while it was I who carried it and risked death to bear it. But that was neither here nor there. I needed a name, and if the King was right about relationships, then I was stuck, for I didn't know the imp's relation-ship to either God or man, and as for his relationship to me? He was my nemesis, but I didn't think that could be a name. Still, I spent that day wandering through the castle and then the town, noting everyone's relationship.

That night when the imp appeared, I gave him three names used by lords of the region.

"Arden, Beauchamp, Deacre"

With every name I put forth, the grin on the imp's face widened, and upon finishing, he reached over me and tightened the swaddling cloth around my baby's neck. Quickly I shoved his hand aside, but nonplussed, he simply said, "Enjoy what time you have," and then he was gone.

Despite being surrounded by men who were quick to tell me what I must and must not do, they had no answers when it came to solving my problem. It was obvious that if I was going to get out of this predicament, then it was going to be by my own means. I sat down to think, and as I did so, it dawned on me that, that's where I'd let myself down all along. I'd allowed others to do the thinking for me. I'd allowed my father to define who I was with his boasting and the King to make unrealistic demands of me, and now I had this little man threatening to take what was rightfully mine.

Thinking back to that third night in the room with the spinning wheel and a pile of straw, I berated myself. Why hadn't I thought to say no? Why hadn't t said to the king, "I've spun one room as agreed. I've spun two because you bullied me into it, but I don't want to be your queen, so I'm not doing another. Whereas I'd spent my first night crying out of fear and the second from frustration, by the third night I should have cried out in anger.

It's easy to grasp at straws, I thought, when that's all you think you have available to you. It's a bitter lesson, but one I now realised was important for me to learn. I'd taken the imp's offer because I thought there were no other options. The same was true when it came to giving the King my hand. By giving in, I'd given up. As I looked back at the choices I'd made, I made up my mind. I stood up and looked in the mirror, and this time instead of seeing a hapless girl, I saw a powerful woman. For the first time, I saw myself not as I was but as I could be.

"No more," I said. "No more relying on others. If anyone is going to save your child, it's you." And that is how I found myself storming out of the castle and into the forest.

There are some that say I came across the imp and overheard his boasts, but the truth is that the fresh air and freedom was what provided me with the answer. It had been before me all the time, but I'd failed to see it. It was in the naming and not in the name. So subtle and now so obvious.

That night when the imp appeared, I was waiting for him. I sat in my chair by the window, staring out at the moonlit sky, singing a lullaby to my little baby girl.

"It's the last night of our little game," he said. "And I hope you have enjoyed it as much as I."

"I'm eager to have it finished," I replied, turning to face him.

"Then let's get on with it," he snapped back at me. "Give me your answers, so I can get what's rightfully mine."

"Oh, you'll get what you deserve," I replied. Then turning to face him, I said, "Is it Kunz?"

He stepped closer. "No."

"Perhaps it's Heinz."

He stepped directly in front of me and held out his hands, but I ignored them. Instead, I stood up and towering over him, I said, "How about I just call you what I think of you, you Rumpled Stilted Skin of a —,"

But before I could finish, he screamed, "What! What did you say?"

Hands that had been stretched out to take my child from me, pulled back. Rage welled up in the little man so that tiny veins in his neck turned purple and his eyes nearly burst from their sockets. "How did you learn that? Who told you? What kind of witchcraft did you employ?" Along with those accusations, he spouted epithets that do not bear repeating while his body shook violently. Terrified, I pushed back against my chair, holding my child tight and then...

Poof! He was gone. Not having gotten his way, he threw a tantrum and disappeared.

Over time, there are those who would say that he stomped his right foot so hard that he sank into the ground up to his waist. Others would claim that he grabbed his left foot and pulled until he tore himself in two. To be honest, I don't know what happened to Rumpelstiltskin, just as most people don't know what happened to me. I suppose they thought that I lived happily ever after in the castle with the King, but that wasn't the case.

When I told the king the whole story, he too was furious. Not because he nearly lost his first child, he was less concerned about that because, as I've already mentioned, she was a girl. No, he was furious that not only couldn't I spin straw into gold, but I had most likely destroyed the one person who could. The marriage was promptly annulled on the grounds of my deception, and my father's mill was confiscated. This angered my father, and he in turn disowned me. And the blacksmith boy who'd given me the ring had another as his wife. I found myself an unmarried woman with a child and no man to protect me. I could have wound up begging in the streets except that I refused to accept the fate that life had doled out to me.

I sought out the moneylender. The one the king had refused to pay as promised and convinced him that the best revenge on the king was to help me become successful. He lent me a modest sum at low interest to start my own spinning business. While I couldn't spin straw into gold, I was still good enough at my craft to turn out unique and beautiful items. I became known far and wide for my artistry and was soon able not only able to support myself and my daughter, but to repay the loan as agreed.

The funny thing is that the imp, the King and even my father had failed to see the worth of a girl. That was the truth I learned in the forest. And in realising that, I realised something else. The pact I made was for my firstborn. The law, which men and imps hold in such high regard, stipulates that the firstborn can only be applied to a male child.

My child, a girl, was not the firstborn, and that is what I planned to tell the imp, except that he didn't hang around to hear my argument. No matter, for it is I who learned the greatest lesson and, in the process, answered my own question.

What's in a name?

It's independence, and it can be spelled in any number of ways. In my case, the sign above my door spells it Spinster but my daughter may choose to spell it differently. She may spell it as Ruler or Academic or Artist or any way she chooses. The only important thing is that she has a choice and that she not be afraid to assert herself.

Chapter 4

MARGRET

"You've spun a fine tale, Beatrice," said Margret. "One that reflects the great changes that came with my generation." She reached over with her hand and, patting Beatrice's said, "Don't get me wrong. Your generation brought in new ideas," she made that little side-to-side movement with her head, "mostly for men, but great ideas, nonetheless. Unfortunately, ideas require action, and that is what my generation did. We acted."

"Are you sure you want to compare the advances of the Age of Enlightenment against that of the Industrial Revolution?" said Ginger. "Wasn't it your era that changed the meaning of spinster from that of a skilled artisan to that of an unmarried woman.?"

"Don't forget to add one that's ugly, prudish and generally undesirable," added Verna.

Margret looked past Ginger to stare straight at Verna. The sarcasm wasn't unusual, but there was something else, something more cutting than usual. Overlooking the undercurrent of whatever was troubling Verna, Margret retorted, with her own sarcasm, "Why Verna, I believe it was your generation that made the term obsolete."

"I blame its demise on Flo's generation," said Ginger. Sitting between Margret and Verna, she seemed keen to keep the peace between the two.

"Well, thank goodness the word spinster has become obsolete," said Flo. "I don't plan to marry, at least not until I'm settled in my career, which isn't likely to happen until I'm in my thirties, maybe even forties."

"For that, you can thank my generation," said Verna. "We made marriage and children an option, not an obligation."

"And yet, you married," said Ginger.

"True," replied Verna, "we promoted free love, open marriages or polyamory, as my daughter Chloe prefers to call it." She raised the tankard and took a long sip.

Chloe's absence and the reason behind it, was obviously troubling Verna, but resting the tankard back on her lap, she continued. "And yet," she stopped to shoot a glance towards Ginger, "for all our options, we still chose to marry."

"And get divorced," quipped Margret, head down and hands busy with her needles and yarn.

"And marry again," said Verna as if there'd been no interruption. "In fact, I'm pretty sure we're the most married and, "nodding in Margret's direction, "the most divorced generation and now we're the most likely to co-habit."

"A term which I might add, you did not invent," said Margret.

"Perhaps not," replied Verna, "but we made it socially acceptable." Holding up the jug that sat on the floor between herself and Flo, she refilled her tankard and asked if anyone else wanted some. When no one replied, she shrugged her shoulders and placed it back on the floor.

Beatrice took advantage of the lull in Verna and Margret's sniping to bring the conversation back to a more intellectual, less volatile discussion about language.

"Margret's point about her generation's impact on our language is an important one. The Age of Enlightenment was all about ideas, grand ideas, but as Margret pointed out, those rights didn't extend to women. Women's rights and the term feminism didn't appear until industrialization."

"Do you really believe that Beatrice," said Ginger. "After all, your treatise on women was widely read."

"And quickly forgotten. No, what really sparked change was not education or idealism; it was women going to work in factories."

"For half the pay," interjected Margret.

"And then coming home to do the child rearing and the housework," continued Beatrice, "I was a lone voice asking why women weren't allowed to be intellectually equal to men, but it was factories that were the great levellers. Factories and their need for workers opened up jobs for women and children because there weren't enough men to fill the demand."

"Beatrice is right," said Margret, "women have always worked and like the spinster in her story, sometimes they earned enough to support themselves but prior to industrialization there was women's work which centred in and around the home, and there was men's work. Sons followed in the footsteps of their fathers just as girls became wives like their mothers. The Industrial Revolution changed everything." She laughed. "Beatrice's generation may have generated a lot of hot air, but mine generated steam, and it was steam that fuelled mechanization, and mechanization gave birth to factories. *Factorium* is Latin for a place of doers, and the Industrial Revolution was the age of doers. New words — train, railway, automobile and horsepower — entered the language. New words were created for the new jobs: factory girl and pieceworker and sweater." Oh, not the kind you wear; that meaning came later. The first sweaters were middlemen who made the workers work harder. They were contractors whose only function was to bully workers into working up a sweat" She finished the row and turned the piece she was working on around. "The term maid, like spinster, shifted its meaning from that of a young, unmarried girl to that of a domestic servant. The wealthy had always had servants, but the Industrial Revolution gave rise to middle-class wives who were financially able to employ household help. While working as a domestic wasn't much better for women, it offered even more opportunities for work outside the home. And since men and women were now as likely to be doing the same or similar jobs, the disparity in pay was obvious."

"Birth, death, taxes and less pay for more work. Some things haven't changed," said Verna.

Ignoring that comment, Margret continued, "The number of women in the workforce during the early days of industrialization is hard to calculate because the census figures didn't list the professions of dependants in the household and wives were considered dependants but by the mid-nineteenth century there were enough women working to cause resentment among men who felt their wages and even their livelihoods were threatened. Like the guilds of an earlier age, they wanted women excluded from particular trades. These new unions sought to have legislation barring women from jobs that were 'unhealthy' for women. Unhealthy! What was unhealthy was women working full time in a factory and then coming home to look after the children and the house while their husbands went to the pub. As for giving women the right to vote, Beatrice's male counterparts argued that women didn't have the mental capacity to vote, but my generation argued that we didn't have the time."

Margret set her knitting on her lap and fingered the blue sash that ran across the white bodice of her dress.

"We wore sashes to let everyone know what we stood for."

"Like creating a brand," said Flo.

"We weren't cattle," said Margret, sounding offended.

"She's using the modern term." said Beatrice. "It means to create a unique image that people associate with a company or, in your case, a movement."

"Oh, sorry, Flo," said Margret. "Yes, wearing a sash branded us as suffragists. And the colour of the sashes was significant." She pulled a skein out of her bag and started the next row, tying in a new colour.

"The English suffragists wore sashes in purple, white and green. Purple for freedom and dignity, white for purity and green for hope. In America, they used the same colours except for Kansas. They changed yellow to gold because they liked sunflowers." Another little shake of the head and another stitch. "Blue, like the one I wear, was localized to Massachusetts, the blue bird state. It was home to Anne Hutchinson, banned in 1630 for preaching to mixed-gender congregations, Abigail Adams, wife of John Adams who told her husband to 'remember the ladies' when they wrote their new laws, and Lucy Stone who is, erroneously, most famous for keeping her maiden name after she married. Then, of course, the first two National Women's Conventions and the Lowell Female Labor Reform Association --."

When Margret paused to catch her breath, Flo said, "Many of those women were also influenced by local women of the Haudenosaunee tribe."

"Who?" asked Margret.

"Iroquois Indians. They were a matriarchal tribe."

"Were they?" asked Ginger.

"I'm sure there was some exchange of information," said Margret," but the movement was basically white working women."

Beatrice glanced towards Flo, who looked like she wanted to say more but decided against it. Meanwhile, Margret continued.

"The suffragists didn't only fight for women's rights either. Many were abolitionists and were instrumental in getting the vote for black men."

"And still the United States didn't give women the right to vote until years after New Zealand, Australia, Finland and the UK had done so," said Verna.

This time, Beatrice interceded.

"Perhaps we should move on to Margret's tale."

Verna started to speak but was silenced by a look from Beatrice - who then realised that she'd done what they railed against most - silencing a sister. But neither Margret, nor Verna noticed. One returned to her drink, the other to her needles. Those needles rarely sat idle. They pushed through one loop, waited for the yarn to embrace one or the other yarn, then the chosen one pulled the yarn through to form the next loop: one row interlocking with the next. The shape and texture dictated by the sequence in which the yarn was manipulated by the needles. Beatrice could tell that the rows were taking on a shape, but its final form was not yet clear. All she knew for sure was that whatever Margret was composing, it was colourful. And so, the needles clicked rhythmically, the rows grew and Margret began garnered everyone's attention.

"When I was small, my mother told me fairy tales. They were meant to entertain but also to teach. When she finished telling the story of Hansel and Gretel, she'd always add–and that's why you should not trust strangers and things are not always what they seem. Verna's generation pooh-poohed women's crafts like knitting, but they failed to appreciate, like the German soldiers, what women are capable of - hiding in plain sight."

She glanced sideways at Ginger; the barest hint of a smile crossed her face.

"During the great war that sent the men into tanks, marching and bombing their way across Europe, women watched and knitted. A knit, a purl, a dropped stitch, a scarf sent in the mail, that's how many seemingly innocent women conveyed details of troops and troop movements."

Margret chuckled as she turned her knitting around to start another row.

"Fairy tales and the older myths warn us time and time again not to judge someone by their outward appearance. It might be a goddess posing as a shepherdess or a house made of gingerbread or an innocent old woman with her knitting. But then again," her needles clacked, "how do you ever know who to trust? We assume so much based on how someone looks or pretends to act. Relationships are a labyrinth we wander into, and there's always the danger that somewhere in the dark recesses of that labyrinth, a monster dwells. Stories are like that. We think they are leading to one place. Then—"

She paused to bite the yarn and reached into her basket to retrieve a skein of a different colour. As she began the new row, needles clicking, she continued.

"We find that the actual story is something completely different. It leads us through twists and turns before revealing its true nature. So, it is with people. Which is why a lot of fairy tales involve not only evil posing as good but good being concealed by rags, or monstrous looks. In those tales, the outward appearance offers no clue to what hides below the surface. The fairy godmother changes Cinderella's rags for a ball gown, and suddenly she's a princess. Bella's love overcomes the curse, and suddenly the beast is a handsome prince. Conversely, the gingerbread house looks delicious, but it's a trap, and Beatrice's story of the imp who offers to help but tricks the maid into making an unconscionable agreement. But some fairy tales offer few clues as to what lesson they try to teach, and the one that I found most difficult to understand when I was young was the princess and the pea."

She turned the knitting around and began a new row.

"On the surface, it seems a silly tale of a girl so sensitive to comfort that she can feel the tiniest irritation, that of a pea under a pile of mattresses, but how is that a test of what it takes to be a Queen. As I grew older, however, I began to understand what the Queen was really looking for, so like the spinner in Beatrice's tale, I think the Queen deserves to give voice to her own story."

The needles fell still as Margret set the knitting on her lap and began.

Chapter 5

TO BE A QUEEN

N OT EVERY WOMAN IS FIT TO BE A QUEEN. I SHOULD KNOW. I come from a long line of monarchs and was taught how to act, how to think, how to sit at the side of a king. The main role, however, the one that can't be taught, is to breed. A queen, even when she has proven herself indispensable to king or country, in the end, is only valued as a brood mare. Her primary function is to gestate the next heir and woe be the woman who fails to do her duty and bear a son. Deportment can be taught. Finery can make the frump look fetching, but what woman can control the whimsy of her womb?

The womb, that idle organ, tucked away in the belly of a woman, so small and insignificant and yet it has the ability to create alliances, provide kingdoms with stability and possibly even tame the beast on the throne. And yet, for all its power, it is under the control of the king. It is his seed that determines X from y and yet failing to bring forth a son is indisputably the fault of the female. Every queen knows this just as she knows that once she has produced all the progeny her body can bear, she is now as superfluous as the womb that no longer functions. Unless. If a woman is not to be relegated to some chamber in the tower, if she is to retain her seat to the left of the throne, then she must learn a new skill. She must become her husband or better still, her son's advisor. For a woman to rule, she must learn how to rule the man who does. This was what I was taught.

My mother was not adept at this business of manipulation. She lived in a time when women were housed in the women's quarters. She was presented to the court by her father. A peace offering to settle disputes over lands to the south. She was young, having only begun to bleed, so what did she know of royal intrigues? Taken to her chambers, she was confirmed a virgin and then presented to my father, the king. He was a widower, without offspring of noble blood, but still in his prime. He took my mother before the wedding and certainly before she was ready. Within the year she was confirmed fecund and they were wed. Thank God they did not wait for the birth for it was I who she birthed and not the son and heir, the king required. A great disappointment but my mother was young and my father made many more visits to my mother's chamber. Another pregnancy, another girl and the whispers began; both of the compassionate and callous kind. Time was on my mother's side but not so that of the king. He had bastard sons, but what he required was an heir. His clock was ticking louder than hers. The third child. How my mother prayed. The more she prayed, the weaker she became. I stood by her side as she grew gravely ill. Was it the child that killed her or the anxiety of its gender? Who knows but, in the end, she did what was necessary. She produced an heir.

A weakling at birth, both slight of build and slow of thought, my mother's last child, was nonetheless, heir. He survived to manhood and rules that kingdom still, although some say, it is his advisors who rule him. I, on the other hand, was sent away. Like my mother, I was bartered in return for an advantageous alliance. Unlike my mother, I was not some naive young thing.

In the women's chambers at my father's house, I was taught lady's skills; embroidery to still my mind and keep my hands employed, dance to show that I knew how to carry myself in public and the lute to show that I had some learning. But my mother and the nurse she employed taught me the skills I would need to escape the confines of the women's quarters. They taught me how to read books written by great thinkers. I was encouraged to use my mind as well as my fingers and my feet and those other parts of the body that men focus their attention on. Most importantly, they taught me, how to shape the minds of men. My mother said that if I was to become more than an extension of a man's reproductive system, I was going to have to stimulate my husband's mind as much as his loins. My mother had never been central to the court and so she passed away, alone and all but forgotten in her lonely tower, except for the words she bequeathed to me.

"Do not let them stick you in the chamber with your maids in waiting. Make yourself indispensable so that if you are put aside, you still retain power."

I did not understand what it meant to be put aside until I had done my primary duty of producing an heir and my husband's eye began to wander.

Over the years, he had many affairs. Some I instigated, pointing out the pretty ones that had no ambition other than a fleeting fancy from the king. They came and went, providing him with diversions to relieve the pressure of the crown. And while he was distracted, I courted his advisors. Not for physical gratification. That a queen must never do. But for power. Men like nothing more than to please a beautiful woman and even as I aged, I retained my beauty. I listened intently to their advice, making the occasional comment, flattering the pompous and engaging the wise. And so, it was when my husband passed away and my son was too young to rule, I was made regent rather than dowager mother. While I might never be king, I had proved that I could rule.

Still the time comes when a young man must face all his responsibilities and produce an heir. My son was in his early twenties when we began a search for his queen. The word was spread far and wide and many a beautiful flower was brought to court and there were a number my son would have gladly wed. I, however, held the final word and was thus able to direct the course of events. If my husband had been in charge, he would have looked at the strategic value of each prospect in the same way my son weighed up their physical attributes. When it comes to choosing women, men think in two dimensions only, power and seduction. I wanted more for my son. I wanted a true queen who would stand side by side with him through the trials and tribulations of what I hoped would be a long reign.

And these were troubled times. Great powers were shifting as old kingdoms fell and young ones rose. The weather was unpredictable and one year's feast barely fed the next year's famine. New ideas. New religions. Unrest roamed the land and many a king, even the wise and just, were overthrown by thugs and henchmen. To be a queen in such times required more than breeding and the ability to produce offspring. A queen in times such as ours required the same leadership qualities as a king.

Alas, there were few princesses raised to be leaders. There were the educated ones, but they lacked real world experience because, unlike their royal brothers, they were kept locked away and safe. Unlike males they were not tested to find and address their short comings. They were, in short, never allowed to fall off the horse and then commanded to get back on. And then there were the women raised to be pawns of their own governments. While I didn't want him to marry a woman who lacked her own identity, I also didn't want him to marry a woman whose lust for power exceeded his own. She needed to be his confidant, his advisor and if necessary, his replacement but I didn't want her to be his rival.

So, one by one the applicants arrived, only to be turned away. My son despaired of my accepting anyone and accused me of refusing to give up my own position of power. Tensions within the castle matched that of those surrounding it. This was the climate into which the would-be queen arrived and matching the mood, the weather had also taken a turn for the worse.

The would-be queen arrived without pomp or ceremony. It was at the end of a long, hot dry summer that had burned the spring's seedlings that the sky split apart, and torrential rains pummelled the parched, cracked earth. The roads in and out of the castle were quagmires, impossible to navigate. Streams overflowed their banks and whole villages were swept away. And in the midst of this mighty storm, came a banging at the door. Such a banging. You would have expected a giant to be demanding entry, yet when the door was flung open, there stood a maid. Her long hair might have been any colour so caked in mud was it. And her clothes, drenched from the rain, clung to her body, revealing her slight build the way a drowned rat's fur showed off its skeleton. Never in my life have I seen such a sorry excuse for a woman and yet when asked her business, she replied that she was a princess come to see the king.

If we had not reached such a desperate point in our search for my son's Queen, I am sure we would have beat her and sent her away. She had none of the hallmarks we had been looking for. My son dismissed her for her lack of beauty and her common dress. The advisors said she was too scrawny to be decent for bearing children and even I wondered what to make of this creature. And yet, there was something in the way she announced her intentions that told me she was more than a scullery maid with visions of grandeur.

"We will put her to the test," I said.

I had her taken to the baths and given a proper cleaning. Once bathed she was given a modest attire, but when she emerged, freshly groomed, she could have been dressed in the finest silks, such was her grace and bearing. No jewels adorned her except the intelligence in her eyes. Relaxed and confident, she entered the room and presented herself, first to the king with a much-practiced curtsey, then turning to me, she bowed in similar fashion. It was obvious she understood the ways of the court, so I allowed her to join us for dinner. I did, however, seat her at one of the lower tables.

I observed her manners closely. Bread passed her way; she acknowledged and partook only her portion. She spoke to those around her, even thanking the serving girl which accounted for why the servants treated her with respect. I noted, then how the table she occupied began to follow her example. There was a jovial, yet respectful presence on that side of the room. Whatever else that girl had, she knew how to set an example that others wanted to follow.

After the meal was cleared, I asked for the musicians. As the dancers took their places on the floor, I kept a close eye on the so-called princess. She was watching each manoeuvre with the intensity of a cat studying a mouse hole. After the first few sets, I told my son to ask her to dance.

"She's not from here so without instruction, she'll make a fool of herself."

"And so, we will see how she handles that."

It was true that she struggled through the first two sets but with each fumble she corrected herself and, more importantly, she improved with each iteration. Now dancing is not a necessity for a queen. On the other hand, learning on the job is. By the end of the night, I was impressed with her ability to adapt, and I could see that my son was beginning to take an interest as well. I had originally told the maids to prepare a room in the servants' quarters but instead I had her escorted to one of the guest suites.

The next morning, I called her to my chambers and asked how she'd slept.

"I can't lie," she said. "I'm afraid I spent the night tossing and turning."

"Was the room not up to your standards," I inquired.

"Quite the opposite, your majesty," she replied quickly. "No, the problem was in my head."

This news shocked me and I began to worry that unfortunately, she was not suitable after all.

"Do you often suffer from headaches?"

"No, I misspoke. It was not a headache that plagued my sleep. It was something the maid told me."

At this I felt the blood rush to my head.

"Was the maid insolent. If she was, I will—"

"No, your majesty, she was courteous and as kind as any lady in waiting."

"Then what?" I demanded.

The young woman sighed.

"Your majesty, if you would indulge me a minute and join me at the window."

I wasn't sure what to make of such a request and so I sat speechless until she walked to the window and said, "Please."

It was the look more than the word that bid me rise and join her. From my rooms, high above the plain, I could see the river, swollen, tearing at the landscape. Trees and debris rushing like unruly children amidst the swirling water.

"The maid told me her house, and all her belongings had been washed away."

"She wasn't alone," I said. "Several villages have been lost. It happens when the rains arrive on the mountains and the river swells. Don't worry. They will rebuild when the water subsides."

"But it is such a waste to constantly lose homes and fields when the river could be tamed."

A terrible fear gripped me and my veins, only moments before raging with fire at the thought of some maid's insolence, turned to ice. Had I invited a witch into my chambers?

"How can one tame a river?" I demanded to know.

She must have noted the change in my demeanour but nonplussed, she continued in a calm and clear voice.

"On my journey here, I passed through many lands. Some mountain places were so steep that the land would have slid away in the gentlest rains had they not sculpted flat areas with rock walls."

She pointed to the gardens at the base of the castle.

"They built structures like your terrace below. These terraces captured and held the water, channelling the overflow into waterways that ran past great wheels that turned the miller's stones to grind the wheat into flour. Perhaps your majesty could send builders to these lands so they too can learn to tame the waters."

I called my ministers and asked her to explain to them what she had seen in her travels. They agreed to send envoys to the lands she told them about. Just as my mother encouraged me to leave the confines of my chamber, I realised the value in this girl's advice to leave the confines of our kingdom. To seek advice and council from others.

That evening my son asked why the woman who called herself a princess looked so tired. I explained that in order to determine if she was a true royal, I had placed a small hard pea under her mattress.

"Is that how you test for a princess?" He exclaimed.

"We are choosing a queen, not a king," I replied. "So, the tests for a woman's suitability to rule is different than for that of a man."

"But a single pea," moaned my son. "That hardly seems adequate."

"Not to worry," I said. "Tonight, I will have them pile on extra mattresses and we'll see how she fares."

At this moment, the confessed princess appeared. I'd sent her one of my silk gowns, laden with jewels and indeed, she looked every bit a royal but looks are not enough by which to judge a queen. If she'd been a man, a simple request to pull a sword from a stone or slay a dragon might have sufficed but I was choosing a wife for my son and that required more than what is required of a king. I required further proof.

The next morning, I had the girl brought before me again.

"And how did you sleep, I asked, although the answer was already apparent."

"Your majesty, I appreciate the extra mattresses but it's not physical discomfort that keeps me awake at night."

"But we've sent envoys to those other kingdoms and have planned works to begin once the river subsides. What worries you now? Is it my son? Is he not paying you the proper attention?"

"Within the castle, all is well," she replied.

I could feel the tension practically bursting from inside her.

"What is it child?"

"After dinner I went to the kitchen to thank the cook and tell her how good the meal was."

"You went to the kitchen?"

"I'm sorry your majesty if I overstepped. It's just that I was so impressed with the meal—"

"We do not go to the kitchen."

I admit that I may have overreacted.

"In future, that is if you have a future, please ask that the cook come to you."

"Again, I apologise your majesty. The rules here are new and strange to me."

"I should think so," I snorted. The girl was about to go when curiosity overrode my displeasure.

"But why, pray tell, did going to the kitchen ruin your sleep?"

She was at the door, her hand resting on the knob. For a moment, I wasn't sure if she would stay or go. Then with an audible sigh, she turned and faced me.

"If your majesty would indulge another of my thoughts."

"Speak."

"The cook told me that the potato harvest is small this year."

"How can that be," I said. "There were plenty served last night."

"Plenty in the castle," she said. "But scarce in the villages."

"Well, perhaps they need to grow more." My voice probably betrayed my lack of understanding.

"They planted plenty but that's the problem."

Once again, I found myself asking for an explanation and once again I was surprised by her response.

"Every year, the peasants plant potatoes in the same fields. Some of the crop developed a blight last year which stayed in the soil and spoiled this year's crop. Worse yet, it has now spread to more fields."

"Blights are an act of God." I waved my hand dismissively. "They come and go. The peasants know that."

"Yes, your majesty, they certainly know when disaster strikes and like you, they are more than willing to blame God."

I crossed myself, for what she was saying bordered on blasphemy. And yet, instead of sending her to the priests, I listened to her explanation.

"It may be God's will that blights exist, but it is the intelligence that that same God gave us, that can teach us how to prevent them."

"And I suppose in your journeys you learned how to farm?" My sarcasm was evident, but her reply had none.

"It's true I have acquired some knowledge in my travels. There is a kingdom on the other side of the mountains that had the same problem, but they changed how they used their fields."

I signalled for her to continue.

"The soil, like humans, grows weak unless it is properly fed."

"But our peasants already feed the soil. They use the waste from the stockyards. Any simpleton knows that."

"Yes, but the soil, like the peasants must vary its labours from time to time and like the peasants the soil also needs a rest in order for the food to take effect. This kingdom I visited, rotated crops from one field to the next and, on the seventh year of the field's work, it was allowed to rest."

"And this keeps crops from failing?"

"No remedy is 100%," she said, "but this rotation reduces loss because the plants are healthier and more resistant to disease."

It was an interesting concept but as Queen, I knew nothing of farming. I called the ministers. They confirmed that indeed the potato harvest was small. Then I had the girl explain this crop rotation and one of the ministers said he used a similar system in his own garden.

"Why have you not mentioned this before," I asked.

"Well," he mumbled. "I suppose because, you never asked me."

I looked the man square in the eyes.

"How many times have you explained the simplest things to me when

I did not ask for such explanations." and cutting his babbling short, put him in charge of educating the peasants who could benefit from his advice.

That night I held a quiet dinner in my chambers. It was for my son, the girl and myself. I quizzed her over dinner, on her upbringing and where her kingdom lay and why she travelled alone.

Her answers were short and to the point. She heralded from a kingdom on the other side of the sea, she explained. Travelling by ship she had seen many lands which she said, explained why it took her so long to respond to our call for princesses.

"Why travel so far and risk so much?" I asked. "You might have been killed. You might have arrived too late. Don't you think you were taking too many risks?"

"I had heard, your majesty, that this kingdom had a wise queen who would embrace a woman of intelligence and skill. I came here because no other kingdom offered me what this one does."

"And what is that?"

"Opportunity to rule equally with the king."

My son stopped, fork in mid-air and looked in my direction.

"You would be my son's equal?"

"I would accept your son on no other terms."

My son started to speak but I raised my hand.

"I think we've said enough for one night. This meal is over."

The girl excused herself and when she was gone my son said, "She has a lot of nerve."

"That, she does but if she can back it up with deeds, we might be wise to give her what she wants.'

"To rule equally along with me."

"Isn't that what we have done all these years since your father died. But before you explode, I have one more test to put her through."

"I should hope it's a difficult one for I'm not sure I'm ready to share any of my power with a wife. No king has ever done that, and I'll not be the first."

"Your father in his own way did exactly that," I replied. "Many the night he left his mistress's bed to seek my council. You didn't know that did you? I suppose few knew." Vexed at myself more than my son, I added, "Perhaps we are the ones that need to change. This girl, as you call her, can't control the weather but she's seen how other kingdoms control its vagaries. She can't prevent famine, but she's brought new ideas about cultivation that may increase our harvests."

"But she's—"

"You could do worse my son," I interjected. "She has much to offer. But tomorrow is another day and she must get through another night."

"Your pea test," he said.

I wasn't sure whether he, like me, used sarcasm to cover his own lack of understanding but I replied, nonetheless.

"Yes, one last tiny pea under a stack of mattresses."

Then I dismissed him and spent the night tossing and turning myself. She had all the hallmarks of a good ruler, but would the kingdom accept a woman who openly commanded a position of authority? If my son was balking at the idea, how many others would resist. Change was never easy but the girl, no the woman, who'd applied to be queen seemed more than capable of selling change. It was a decision I nearly put off because of the news that arrived in the morning.

The plague! No other word struck fear into so many hearts. The throne room was in turmoil. The kingdom to the south had reported deaths and now everyone agreed that the court should retreat to the mountains in the north. Amid this turmoil, the princess appeared.

"I have no time for you today," I said. "Besides, you look exhausted."

"Last night I heard the rumours, and I could not sleep for fear they were true."

"True, they are and we must make ready to depart."

"And leave your kingdom unprotected?"

"What do you mean?"

"You have enemies who will strike once they know you are weak. You must stay."

"But the plague."

"Can be contained."

For once, her voice was commanding. In fact, she spoke so loudly that the room suddenly stilled.

"Listen," she said. "The plague travels from person to person so first we must contain those who are infected. Send out heralds to say that at the first sign of the disease in any village, that the entire village is to be quarantined."

"How," asked my son, "can we stop everyone from leaving?"

"You will your majesty," she replied. "On pain of death. If they do not quarantine themselves, tell them that all in the village will be put to death and the village raised to the ground."

"But that's insane," he replied. "Why would that threat keep them in place when hunger, if not the plague, would drive them out."

"Because you will give your solemn word as king to supply them with food and any necessary supplies. Tell them that food will be dropped at the perimeter but at the same time, proclaim that anyone trying to leave will be killed and their body burned with no thought of a Christian burial."

I could see the confusion in my son's eyes. The girl was right. To leave the castle unprotected was to expose the kingdom to invasion but to keep the villages quarantined relied on a level of trust between monarch and subject. Would they obey was the true test of him as a leader. The Queen in me wanted to step forward with my own counsel but the mother held firm. The decision was now his.

"And there's another thing."

The girl was now the centre of everyone's attention.

"The plague is carried by rats!"

"And I suppose you would have me command them as well."

"No, my lord." She stood tall and commanding, herself. "I would have you send cats to those villages."

"Cats!"

"Yes, get your hands on as many cats as possible. That's how we contained the plague on the ships."

The ministers looked at my son. My son looked at me, and I looked at the woman who was now dressed in travelling clothes, a sword on her hip. I suddenly realised she might be planning to leave even as she was advising us to stay.

"We will adjourn to my chambers and consider your council, " said my son. Then the action moved to another room and there was only the girl and I left.

"Why are you dressed like that?" I asked. "Are you planning to flee the plague?"

"No milady. I came to wait for your answer. For the last three nights I have provided you and your son with good counsel so by now you must realise that my wisdom and experience are worth more than a king's ransom. I came here because I heard this kingdom understood the value of a person, regardless of gender, but if I'm not to rule equal to your son then I have other places to be."

This girl who'd shown up penniless and bedraggled was now a woman issuing ultimatums.

I called for my son because his answer, like the decision about the future of our kingdom lay in his hands. The princess had convinced me that she was truly a queen but the final decision lay with the king for he would have to adapt and only he knew if he was ready for such a woman to be his queen.

Chapter 6

INTERMISSION

"*L*EAVING IT UP TO A MAN," SAID VERNA. "NO WONDER IT TOOK so long for women to get the vote."

"You know the phrase, you can lead a horse to water--," said Margret, "well, we wanted the horse to drink while you wanted it to drown."

The others laughed as Margret returned to her work, a wry smile barely visible.

Not to be outdone by Margret, Verna turned to Flo. "What do you think, Flo? Did you think Margret's tale was about women needing men's endorsement?"

Flo thought for a minute.

"I get that the king has the final say. After all, even if the Queen had a lot of influence, it was still the King who had the power, so I get that part of the story, but what I still don't get is the pea."

Margret gave an exasperated sigh and set down her spoon. "The pea is a metaphor."

"But a metaphor for what?"

Ginger jumped in. "The Queen is looking for a woman who picks up on the small things, even the things that people try to hide or cover up. A good leader picks up on the subtle things. But that's why men and women should work together, because they have different skills."

"Okay, I think I understand, but why all the tests? Isn't one enough?"

"Everyone seems to forget that suffragists had more than one item on their agenda. Our protests weren't only for the women's vote. We worked to abolish slavery—"

"Ending slavery didn't abolish discrimination, though, did it?" said Verna.

"Do you really want to go there, either of you?" said Flo. Her voice was light, almost jesting, but there was an undercurrent of repressed hostility as well. "Neither of you accomplished much for black women and absolutely nothing for indigenous women. Earlier I mentioned the Haudenosaunee to you, Margret, and you shrugged it off. You might know them by other names, Mohawks, Oneidas, Onondagas, Cayugas and Senecas or maybe you just called them Iroquois. Whatever you called them, the earliest American suffragettes learned a lot about women's rights from them. They had what women wanted, a real say in how their tribe was governed. The Seneca Mothers of the Nation were involved in the writing of their own constitution, and I might add the Oneida women's clothing, those loose-fitting trousers, probably inspired the bloomers I expect Margret is wearing under that skirt. And Verna, I wouldn't get too cocky either. Your feminist leaders probably didn't even realise the ways in which they failed black women. White feminists were only interested in women's issues, black men were railing against racism, and there, caught up and left out of both issues, were black women. As for indigenous Americans, like so many other countries that white people colonized, their children were being taken away and sent to boarding schools or missions so they could be anglicized, but what it was really saying is, your culture isn't valuable."

Flo fell silent. As quickly as her diatribe started, it stopped, leaving behind an awkward pause. Finally, Beatrice said, "Thank you, Flo. We all have our blind spots, and it helps to be reminded of them from time to time."

Ginger, who'd thought about the black maid she employed when her and her husband still lived in the city, was also eager to move onto another topic, so she said, "I agree Flo, the battle only achieves its objective when all work for a common goal. But let's get back to the suffragettes," she turned to Verna. "Your generation thinks that Margret and her sisters in their feminine dresses and pretty sashes calmly marched through the streets, but they battled for the vote with bombs. They were imprisoned, and some died. They were labelled enemies of the state."

"Deeds, not words," said Margret nodding her head as her needles resumed their clicking.

"As for you, Margret," Ginger continued. "For all your protests, peaceful and otherwise, it was war and women's involvement in it that won suffrage for women."

"Not true," said Margret. "New Zealand gave women the vote in 1893."

"But not the right to run for Parliament until 1919," said Ginger. "A year after the first great war ended."

"And South Australia gave women the vote in 1894," continued Margret, ignoring Ginger's comment.

"While excluding indigenous, Asians and islanders," said Flo.

"My point is," continued Ginger, "that women didn't gain respect as equals until they engaged in the male activity of warfare. And don't get me wrong, I'm a pacifist, but I think women on the front lines as nurses and behind the lines on farms and in munitions factories showed politicians that women were truly equal."

"If I recall correctly, you worked as a nurse on the front lines," said Margret.

"Indeed, I did."

"And yet, after the war, those same politicians that you suggest were so generous as to give you the opportunity to run for government office, sent you back to your lives as housewives and mothers. If war was so liberating, why did you, as someone who'd trained as a nurse before the war, give up your profession for domesticity?"

"Oh, Margret, you know I had my reasons."

Margret, having made her point, searched through her bag until she found the skein she wanted, then settled back to start a new row with the new colour. "And in future, could you please use the word suffragist?"

"Isn't that what I said?"

"No, you said suffragette."

"Suffragist, suffragette, what's the difference? They're both words that mean the same thing."

"Words are important, Ginger. Inside every word is buried some grain of history. Take the word clue. It comes from the word clew which means a piece of string or yarn. In the story of the labyrinth and the Minotaur, Ariadne gives her lover Theseus a clew, so he can find his way out again?"

"Who's Ariadne and the other one, her lover?" asked Flo.

Margret sighed. "Don't they teach the Greek classics anymore? Theseus was the hero in the story because he kills the minotaur but it was Ariadne who gave him a ball yarn to keep track of the way out of the labyrinth. My point is that if we follow the clues, we can find our way back to what words really imply. Males who supported women's rights called themselves suffragists, but we were called suffragettes. It was intended to say we were smaller and less significant."

"I get it," said Ginger. "Like kitchen and kitchenette or cigar and cigarette."

"Or novel and novelette," added Verna.

"I think you mean novella," corrected Margret.

"No," said Verna in an uncompromising tone. "You have the short story, then the novelette, then the novella, then the novel. It's all based on word counts."

"And what do you call something that's longer than a novel?" asked Ginger, trying to lighten the mood.

"Proust's In Search of Lost Time," quipped Verna. "At just over 1.2 million words, it is undoubtedly the longest work ever published."

"In English," corrected Flo as she poked the fire. "The Mahabharata at 1.8 million is even longer."

Flo's comment was another reminder that feminism, for all its talk of inclusion, was still relatively Eurocentric.

"You've been very quiet, Beatrice," said Flo. "What did you think of Margret's tale?"

During the exchange, Beatrice had been listening, but she'd had also been keeping an eye on Verna. The high heels lay on the ground, toppled over and neglected like a child's toys. And the outlandish clothes were equally askew. The skirt had ridden up, and the sweater had slipped down over one shoulder. Beatrice had witnessed Verna change fashions faster than she changed husbands, and each change of fashion represented a change in attitude. So what was Verna hoping to project with this new outfit? On a younger woman, it might have appeared appealing, but on a woman Verna's age, it smelled of desperation.

"Beatrice?" Flo reached over and touched her knee. "Are you okay?"

"I'm fine," she said reassuringly. "But I think we are all in need of food to help absorb the wine we've been drinking."

Chapter 7

SUPPER

"Nothing brings people together better than the smell of something delicious, so Flo, what have you prepared for us?" asked Margret, lifting the lid on the crock pot.

"It's something my father taught me to cook. It's like your English stew but with some additional spices."

"You know Flo, you've never talked much about your family."

"There's not much to say. My mother comes from one place and my father from another. I'm a bit like this stew, a combination of many different ingredients."

Indeed, the aroma of a warm stew had pervaded the room, but as they gathered around the circular dining table, Beatrice noticed there was an extra chair, the one that had no place setting. Except for Margret's comment at the beginning of the evening, no one had mentioned Chloe. Even Verna, who had an opinion on everyone and everything, who was in the habit of referring to her daughter sarcastically as Superwoman, hadn't so much as mentioned the missing woman. The last time they'd all met up, Beatrice remembered that Chloe had been sullen and rebellious. She'd chalked it up to the way Verna chided her daughter for not being more interested in feminism, but then Flo had taken Beatrice and Margret aside and told them about Chloe's problems at home. Her husband, feeling pressured at work, blamed what he referred to as 'those DEI initiatives' for his stagnant wages and lack of promotions. He figured someone had to take the blame, and Chloe, who was doing well in her career, seemed an obvious target. Margret had said violence against women was nothing new, but Flo said that the problem was growing. She blamed the increasing harassment of women, particularly career women, on men who felt they were an endangered species.

"The problem is that women have adapted to a changing world faster than men, and I think it's only going to get worse as automation and now AI, take over more and more jobs."

But for now, they were all gathered around the table, remarking on the unusual, but no less inviting aromas, while on the other side of the large window, the wind whipped branches against each other. It was a stark reminder that while they were here in this comfortable room with its convivial atmosphere - despite the occasional outbursts - outside, the storm was increasing in its violence.

"Stew is perfect on a night like this," said Margret, taking a seat next to Beatrice. "I didn't think her generation knew how to cook. At least, not something tasty."

Ginger and Flo, taking seats next to each other, were sharing a private joke, while Verna, sitting on the other side of Beatrice, remained quiet. While the others talked and ate, Verna ignored her spoon while the tankard remained in constant use. As Verna reached across the table for the jug to refill it, Beatrice stayed her hand. "Flo's gone to a lot of trouble. At least try a bite."

"You should have warned me," she said, her brow furrowed as if wrestling with a difficult math problem, and her lips drawn tight. In the bright light of the dining room, Verna looked older, more worn out. The cheeky Verna, who was always ready with a sharp comment or a cutting remark, was withdrawn. Chloe and Verna, so connected, so alike, and yet -

Beatrice started to ask what she was supposed to warn Verna about, but when she looked into the younger woman's eyes, she found the answer was already there. Whether it was in response to Flo's accusations of negligence or Chloe's absence or maybe just the fact that she was growing old and was ill-prepared to face that; whatever it was, Verna's eyes expressed what words couldn't. In those eyes, Beatrice saw reflected her own joy, pain, hope, and despair. But also, something else. They were the eyes of a woman who'd lived in a golden age, only to discover that none of it had any value. She'd led women into a world that offered more opportunities than ever, a world that experienced sweeping changes in technology, medicine, lifestyles, a world where aspect of the world was captured, digitized and exposed, where the oceans were explored and exploited, where space was conquered then populated with junk. She'd witnessed family farms being gobbled up by BigAg conglomerates that grew more food but left nothing in the soil for the next generation. And it was women who'd been equal participants in all these changes. They'd invented, cured, designed and managed them. Instead of changing the world to adopt more feminine values, men had changed women to be more masculine. The women of Verna's generation fought in combat and helped make space the new frontier. No longer could the accomplishments and the failings of humanity be blamed on men; women were complicit, as well. And what had it all been for? Verna's generation had the right to vote, but had a woman been elected President in a country that was supposed to be a beacon of hope for the rest of the world? Verna had won the right to own real estate in her own name, and her investments had paid off handsomely, but her daughter couldn't afford to buy a home because speculation made ownership unaffordable. Verna had opened the doors of universities to women, but now they were saddled with the same crippling debt as their male counterparts. An Earth in crisis, rising costs, stagnant wages, a generation of disaffected men and more and more conflicts daily, was this Verna's true legacy?

"If it's any consolation," said Beatrice, "we've all burdened our children with our progress. Chloe will come to understand this herself one day. Now come and eat up. The night's not yet over."

Verna dropped her head on Beatrice's shoulder. No tears. No sobs. But the movement caught Flo and Ginger's attention and they stopped talking. Even Margret stopped mopping up stew with her bread. The lights flickered, and in the silence, the first raindrops splattered against the windowpane.

Aging wasn't only about growing old, thought Beatrice as Verna's head grew heavier on her shoulder. It was about looking in the mirror and seeing who you were - once the mask of youth was stripped away. It was about coming to terms with desire by letting go. Lovers, wealth, even ideas - aging brought with it the reality that nothing is ever truly ours. We think we can acquire these things, pass them on to our children, somehow create immortality through legacy, give our life meaning. But there is always the suspicion lurking in the deep recesses of our minds that life has no meaning except what we give to it. Religion, that great promise of immortality, comforts some. Legacy, the desire to live on in memory, is just as elusive. It lasts for a time, but it too fades. As Verna lifted her head, Beatrice looked around the table. These were the women who kept her alive, but in another season or two, others would sit around this table, and her place would pass to someone more up to date. There was no such thing as immortality. The ability to dream of it, long for it, that was life's little joke.

Verna took a deep breath, even as the others held theirs. The rain beat harder against the window. In the other room, the fire dwindled, and the shadows lengthened.

Then, a loud bang made everyone jump. Something heavy had smashed against the window, and Flo jumped up to check that nothing was broken and returned to say that everything was okay. Giggles of relief followed, and Verna picked up her spoon and together she and Beatrice finished their meal.

Chapter 8

GINGER

Back in their places around the fire, it was Ginger's turn to tell a tale. "Over supper, Flo and I were talking about fashion and apparently, the 50s are back in vogue," she said.

"As is the idea of the trad wife," said Flo.

They both laughed as Margret said, "What on earth is a trad wife?"

"Think of it as Supermom meets traditional wife," replied Ginger.

"Yep," said Flo. "The 50s stay at home woman on steroids."

"On steroids? Are these words in the dictionary?"

"Maybe not your dictionary," said Flo, to which Verna added, "Really, Margret, you must keep up with the times."

Margret humphed in reply and exchanged the yarn she'd been working with for another. "Well, let's get on with it then."

Ginger put her hands behind her head and crossed her ankles.

"I know that when I first invited myself into this little group, there were some objections."

Beatrice remembered those discussions very well. It was all about who did and didn't represent women and what feminism was all about. Margret argued that feminism was about the struggle for political equality. That it was essential for women to lobby for laws that protected and ensured women's rights. But Beatrice had pointed out that she was known for her writings on women's intellectual equality, not suffrage, although she conceded that political power was probably implied. And Verna, for once, had agreed with Margret, saying that Ginger's generation had set the feminist movement back by 50 years. Beatrice didn't quite agree. They hadn't destroyed the gains made by the suffragists; they had simply taken a bit of a breather, and given the extraordinary times they lived through, a break was understandable. But, it was Ginger, herself, who'd made the most compelling case.

"You say feminism is about giving women a choice. Well, that shouldn't exclude women who choose to be full-time carers. Whether they are mothers or unpaid workers in the community, they are just as important as someone who earns a wage. Why should a homemaker be any less of a feminist than someone who works outside the home?"

She pointed out that movements, especially those like the women's movement, that spanned generations, had to consider events that were outside the movement, and the second world war was just such an event. "It wasn't only men who wanted to forget the horrors of the past by recreating an image of what they thought life had been like before. Yes, we were sold a false dream, but we wanted it to be true. How badly, we wanted it to be true. We saw pictures of entire cities obliterated and we wanted to hide in our nice, safe, little suburbs. My mother had been born into a world that had seen wars fought over everything from boundary lines to battles to end slavery, but none of those wars compared to the war that was supposed to end them all. She said goodbye to one husband, and they gave her back a different one - one that had been changed by the war. The man who came home was broken both within and without. My mother cared for him - despite the way he fluctuated between being distant and being aggressive - until his liver gave out and he mercifully died. When he couldn't work, she took in washing. When other women went to work, she looked after their children. And during the Depression, she was joined by even more women who found themselves doing the same. Not because their husband's died but because, unable to support their families, they simply took off. It's fine to talk of grand ideas and political power but women, through wars and economic downturns, are the ones most likely to support their children. What is feminism about if it isn't about standing by other women?"

Now that it was Ginger's turn to tell a story, Beatrice wondered what version of an old fairy tale she was likely to tell. Would it be a story of sacrifice for love, like the Little Mermaid? For Ginger's husband had gone away to the second great war and come home whole on the outside and broken on the inside. Both Beatrice and Margret knew how Ginger had given up her nursing career to move to the country so that he could heal.

Or perhaps, she might tell a variation of the German fairy tale like The Waters of Life. It was about an old king who sends his sons to search for the only thing that will keep him from dying, the mythical waters of life. The twist is that the youngest son, the one who finds the healing water, has it taken by the older sons? Healing, sacrifice, and a man taking credit for something he hadn't earned - It was a good start for a feminist fairy tale - but would Ginger pick up a theme like that?

While Beatrice pondered, Ginger reached under her chair and pulled out a box. She opened the lid, and there was a collective sigh. Ginger's tarts were famous. As she passed the box to Margret, she said, "When my husband returned from the war, he wanted nothing more than for me to take care of the house and the children. So, we moved to the country. It was a small-town miles from a hospital and doctors. It wasn't too bad. We could get there in an emergency, but pregnant women didn't consider themselves an emergency. They rarely took themselves to hospitals, so I took up midwifing. Like my husband, I needed to know I had not just a purpose but a position in the community."

Margret chose a cherry tart and handed the box to Beatrice while Ginger continued. "After a while, he started to resent my being called away at all hours of the day and night - You don't have to do this, he'd say - as I rushed around the house gathering my things. Then as I kissed him good-bye, he'd grumble - Half these women can't even pay you - to which I would say - I thought you didn't want your wife to work for money. His arguments would follow me out the door and to the gate, where his hand would hold the latch, and he would remind me that the whole point of his supporting the family was so that I'd stay home."

"And did you?" asked Flo, taking the box Beatrice passed over to her after selecting the other cherry tart.

"No, I'd kiss his cheek and take his hand off the latch while I reminded him that he had his duty as a man and I had mine as a woman."

The box moved to Verna, who passed it on without taking one.

"Are you sure?" said Ginger, taking the box, while Verna responded by refilling her tankard and said, "Don't worry about me. Just get on with your story or we'll be here till dinner tomorrow."

Ginger selected a tart and set the box back on the floor. "In the early years, when our children were small, it wasn't easy, but we made it work."

She fingered the tart, took a bite, then continued, "Before I left this afternoon, I said that I thought my sisters needed me more than ever. And not just for my tarts." She smiled as she shoved the last bite into her mouth.

Meanwhile, Beatrice noticed how Verna glanced down at the box with its two remaining tarts.

Wiping the crumbs off her hands, Ginger continued, "So instead of some grand story about heroic deeds, I thought I'd tell a tale about a humble female. The sort of person who makes the seemingly insignificant but no less important decisions that keep a house running. The problem I had was figuring out what kind of test my heroine would have to deal with."

Her smile widened, spreading across her face, and her eyes sparkled.

"When Flo was telling me about trad wives, I thought, what's the difference between a female with a trade and a trad wife?"

She looked around the room.

No one answered.

"It's the letter e. Otherwise, they're both just people working at creating what Flo calls their brand. Homemaker is a job just like any other so instead of calling my story the Fussy Hussy, as I originally intended, I've decided to call it Trade Without the E."

Margret brushed the crumbs from her lap and pulled out her knitting while Flo poked the fire. Outside, the wind was whipping icy rain against the big window, and on the other side of the glass, Beatrice saw how the ice covered the last of the flowers and painted the branches of the trees with icicles. and inside, Verna, refilled her tankard as Ginger swallowed the last bite of her tart and with a wink in Flo's direction, began her tale.

Chapter 9

TRADE WITHOUT THE E

PULLING HER BEST APRON OFF ITS PEG, MAMA BEAR SWORE. IT
wasn't something she'd done before, but she'd heard Papa Bear do it
and decided that after today, she'd earned the right to let off steam herself.

Damn! Damn! Damn!

As she swore, she stomped her feet and pummelled the wall of the
pantry with her massive paws till the dishes rattled and threatened to fall.
She filled her lungs with air and pushed it through her massive larynx and
hyoid bone so that her low resonance vocalisations thundered through her
internal air sacs, then emerged triumphant into the surrounding air. It felt
wonderfully relaxing to give voice to her rage for once, and now that it was
out; she felt much better.

She slipped the apron over her head and tied it behind her back.

The morning had started like any other. Then everything had been
just so. The outside world, the one Papa Bear complained was going to the
dogs - an animal he detested -had been none of her concern. It was Papa

Bear who read the morning paper and muttered, 'What is this world coming to', while Mama Bear cooked their morning porridge. It was Papa Bear who came home from work grumbling about the breakdown in family values while Mama Bear made sure the cushions on his chair were just so and Baby Bear was fed and bathed and ready for bed. It was Papa Bear who growled about how no one respected him for his brute strength anymore as he scoffed down the dinner Mama Bear had spent hours cooking. And it was Papa Bear who sank into his comfy chair and fell asleep while Mama Bear washed up the evening dishes and made sure the house was just so for her to do it all again the next day.

But today, the outside world, the one Papa Bear claimed to protect her from, had broken in, and her world that had always been just so, was now all topsy-turvy. And worst of all, it was Papa Bear who'd opened the door and invited all these strangers in.

Strangers with strange ideas, she humphed as she filled the sink with hot soapy water and snapped on her rubber gloves. What went on outside was none of her business, just as this house, her den of domesticity, where she kept everything just so, was nobody's business but hers. You would think by now that Papa Bear understood that and would respect her domain as much as she respected his.

She placed the bowls in the warm sudsy water; Papa Bear's first, then hers and finally Baby Bear's; a reminder of how her day should have been, warm and comfortable. And that was how it started - bowls on the table, chairs waiting for them to sit and the beds tidied - everything just so. But then, Papa Bear proclaimed –

"My porridge is too hot. Let's go for a walk to let it cool down."

Mama Bear had wanted to disagree because, first of all, his porridge was the same temperature it was every day and secondly, because she knew that by the time they returned, hers would be too cold. But it was never wise to contradict Papa Bear, and so the breakfast that she'd set on the table, just so, was left, while they went for a walk.

Even now, she was still angry over that walk, but it was Papa Bear who made all the fuss when they got home. As she washed the dishes, the wind snapped the freshly washed tablecloth that was hanging on the line, and Mama Bear looked outside to see that everything was still just so. The clothes drying were waving in the wind, the way Papa Bear had waved his great paws when he realised someone had taken a bite of his porridge.

"It's only a bite," she'd said in an attempt to calm him down.

"A bear's home is his castle!"

His voice, filled with rage, shook the walls of their tidy cottage so badly that Mama Bear had to catch the porridge bowls from toppling to the floor. She understood his distress. She really did. All their bowls had been touched, but if anyone deserved to be upset, it was Baby Bear. That bowl had been licked clean. And then there was the whole thing about the chairs.

"Someone's been sitting in my chair."

It was true. The cushions Mama Bear had placed just so were all askew. But at least their chairs were still intact. It was Baby Bear's chair that lay in pieces. Mama Bear could reassemble it, but it would never be just so. Like the ideas Baby Bear sometimes brought home from school. Ideas that questioned the old ways, and no matter how Mama Bear tried to undo the damage, she worried that things might not always be just so.

And then Baby Bear had screamed from the bedroom. Papa Bear, seeing his bed mussed up, roared –

"Someone's been sleeping in my bed."

Well, that was obvious. Someone had slept in hers as well, but she was the one who'd tidied them in the first place, and she was the one who'd have to make them just so again. If anyone should have been upset, it should have been her, but then Baby Bear pointed out that the culprit was still asleep in bed. She was only a little girl, about the same age as Baby Bear. Now, Mama Bear agreed that the girl had no right to be there, but Papa Bear shouldn't have reacted the way he did. It was only a child after all. If it had been up to her, she would have scolded the child and sent her home, but Papa Bear let his temper get the best of him. He roared his most ferocious roar, scaring the child half to death. While it was the girl who'd caused all the fuss, Mama Bear couldn't help thinking that Papa Bear had blown it all out of proportion. Wasn't it enough that the peace and order of her home had been shattered and Baby Bear had been traumatized, but Papa Bear made things worse by scaring the child? Then he went off to work, leaving her to put the house back, so it was just so and, as it happened, deal with the aftermath of his tirade. And what an aftermath there was!

She had just reassembled Baby Bear's chair and straightened the cushions on the chairs so that they were just so and remade the beds, so they too were just so, and was about to do the washing up, when there was a knock at the door.

It was the police responding to Papa Bear's report of a break-in. Instead of sitting down with a calming cup of chamomile tea and a spoonful of honey, she'd found herself answering the detective's questions. Why had they gone out for a walk? If they locked the door, why had they left the window open? Was the girl armed? Had they feared for their safety? And all the while, the other uniformed police were tracking dirt in on their shoes and messing up the cushions on the chairs and moving the beds to check for prints. And, of course, she'd been compelled to offer the detective tea, which meant even more washing up. And she still hadn't had hers.

Which was why it was nearly lunchtime before the house was once again just so and she was able to put the water on for tea. That's when there was another knock at the door.

If she'd known who the woman was, she might never have opened it. But peering through the curtains, Mama Bear saw a rather plain-looking woman neatly dressed in a conservative suit. Noting the lack of make-up and the hair hastily pulled back and held in place with a scrunchy, Mama Bear decided that the woman must be one of those modern women. The ones Papa Bear referred to as radical feminists.

"These females are taking our jobs and lowering our wages."

The woman on their doorstep was wearing a suit, and Papa Bear wore a suit, so this confirmed her suspicions that the woman was a radical, so she told her to go away.

"But I came to talk to you about this morning's incident with my daughter."

This was the girl's mother?

Given that the child was, in Papa Bear's estimation, a juvenile delinquent, Mama Bear had assumed the child came from a broken home; one where the mother worked some menial job rather than staying home and teaching her child how to behave and where the absence of a father meant there was no paternal discipline. But this woman didn't fit Mama Bear's expectations of a single mom.

She opened the door. "If you've come to apologise, there's no need. It's a police matter now."

"I know," said the woman, "but I thought we could sort things out between ourselves. May I come in? I've brought cake."

Mama Bear's initial thought was to slam the door in the woman's face but the smell of the cakes made her stomach grumble, and she was overdue for her morning tea, and well, she hesitated just so, and the woman took that as an invitation and walked in.

The nerve! thought Mama Bear as she followed the woman into the kitchen. The kettle was whistling on the stove, and the woman said, "I see my timing is excellent. Do you have black tea? I don't take milk or sugar."

Mama Bear looked at the newly washed cups. Papa Bear's was quite large, and Baby Bear's was too small. Hers, however, was just right, and indeed, it had been the one she gave the detective and had just finished washing so she could use it for herself. Sighing, she put the teabag in her cup and added hot water. Her chamomile tea would have to wait.

Meanwhile, the woman was talking as if they were old friends.

"I'm afraid Goldilocks can be a bit of a handful. She's so adventurous, you see." The woman said, adjusting the cushions as she settled into Papa Bear's chair.

"Adventurous," snorted Mama Bear. "Is that what they call climbing through an open window and stealing someone else's porridge these days?"

"She's only seven, but I assure you she's had a firm talking to and, of course, my husband and I are happy to compensate you. The police said something about a broken chair."

Mama Bear slapped the cup on the table but otherwise didn't respond. If you can't say something nice, her mother had taught her, then say nothing at all. Not that the woman noticed. She was fiddling with the cushion in Papa Bear's chair.

"This chair is quite firm," she said as she grabbed the cushion off Baby Bear's chair. "That's Papa Bear's chair," said Mama Bear. "He likes it firm because, as head of the family, he must be commanding. It's the same reason that I like mine soft. My job is to make the home warm and comforting."

Mama Bear thought she'd made her point, but the woman simply responded, "In our house, all the chairs are the same."

"Even for your little girl?"

"Well, the chair is a bit big for Goldilocks, but in time, she'll grow into it."

Mama Bear stole a glance at Baby Bear's chair. She'd been so happy to have reassembled it just so but now she had the uncomfortable feeling that it looked rather childish. Still, it was a mother's role to guide her child gently but firmly into their proper role, and sometimes that meant sitting in a chair that no longer fit.

The woman must have noticed how Mama Bear stared nostalgically at Baby Bear's chair because she quickly said, "It's so tempting to keep them young and innocent, isn't it? We hope nothing bad will ever happen to them, but, as we know, the world can be a dangerous place, and children must be taught to deal with that."

Before Mama Bear could respond, Goldilocks' mother opened the box containing the cakes. The smell had been inviting, but the look of them was even more enticing. They were dripping in honey and sprinkled with pistachios. As Mama Bear set plates and forks on the table, Goldilocks' mother apologised for bringing store-bought cakes instead of bringing something homemade.

"Between work and home, I'm afraid I don't have time to bake, but you must do a lot of baking. When I came in, the first thing I noticed was that your house smells of cinnamon." She placed a cake on each of the plates. "No wonder Goldilocks' was tempted to come in."

If the cakes hadn't distracted her, Mama Bear might have said that the aroma of cinnamon was hardly an invitation to break into someone's house, but instead she took the cake in her massive paw and shoved it into her mouth. The woman ate hers in smaller bites, but in the end the result was the same. Mama Bear licked her paw while Goldilocks' mother licked her fork.

"If you're too busy to bake," asked Mama Bear, "perhaps that's why Goldilocks was wandering around looking for something to eat?"

"Oh, Goldilocks has breakfast," said the woman. "She usually has a bowl of cereal or toast with jam."

Mama Bear was silently congratulating herself for being the kind of mother who made sure her family started the day with a hot and nutritious breakfast when the woman said, "My husband is responsible for making breakfast because I often work nights. I'm a surgical nurse at the hospital."

Mama Bear wasn't sure which was more startling. The fact that the woman worked nights or that her husband cooked.

"If you work nights, who cooks dinner?"

"Oh, Harry, that's my husband. He works from home and likes to cook. He says it's his special time with Goldilocks. Unfortunately, neither of them likes to clean up after themselves. That they leave to me."

Then, the woman asked a most peculiar thing.

"Do you work, Mrs Bear?'

"Work? Of course, I work. I make sure the house is just so and—"

"I mean, do you have a job?"

"Oh, you mean work outside the home. Oh, no. Taking care of my family and the house is a full-time job."

"I thought so," said the woman. "Your house is so tidy." There was a wistfulness in the woman's voice. "In some ways I envy you."

Mama Bear, who'd just placed the dishes in the sink, sat back down.

"Don't get me wrong," said the woman. "I like my job. I think I'd go crazy if I stayed in the house all day by myself, but it's tiring working a full-time job and then having to come home to housework. Sometimes, I think Harry gets to choose the jobs he likes, while I have to do the rest."

Mama Bear felt compelled to say something.

"We bears are very traditional. The males work outside the home, and the females look after the house and the little ones, but I know what you mean about feeling tired. My husband works eight hours a day, but my day begins before his and ends after he's gone to bed. Still, I don't think I'd like a job. Papa Bear says its repetitious and boring."

"That's what my mother said about housework," said Goldilocks' mother.

"But isn't your job boring and repetitious?" asked Mama Bear.

"Many days feel like that, but the paycheck makes it worthwhile. But what about you? Don't you feel like you're not appreciated?"

"Why do you think I feel unappreciated?"

Mama Bear thought she sounded a bit defensive, probably because that was how she felt, but if the woman noticed, she didn't comment. She simply said, "Because you don't get paid."

Ah, money, thought Mama Bear. The outside world put a lot of store in money. Papa Bear complained about who was earning more and who was earning less.

"Papa Bear says females are willing to work for less money than males. Doesn't that make you feel less appreciated?"

"I never thought of it in those terms, but it does bother me that I earn less. On the other hand, I suppose I'm glad to have a job that pays as much as it does. But money aside, don't you get lonely staying at home?"

Mama Bear thought about this. Certainly, there were times when the house felt small, but then she would go to the shops. But it hadn't always been so isolating being a housewife. Out loud she said, "There used to be more bears in this area. My mother would get together with the other mama bears, and they would forage for berries or honey. Now, I just go to the shops and buy what we need."

"I know what you mean. My mother stayed at home while my father worked, but I didn't want to be like her."

"Why not?" asked Mama Bear.

"I think because I felt my mother wasn't happy being a housewife."

A terrible thought was forming in Mama Bear's head. Sometimes she felt lonely at home by herself. Was she in danger of waking up one day and thinking she didn't want to be a housewife anymore? She shoved the thought aside. She liked being a housewife, and besides, she wasn't trained for anything else.

Again, the woman must have read her thoughts because she said, "Goldilocks says Baby Bear is lucky to have a stay-at-home mom. That's why Goldilocks was so excited by the invitation."

"Invitation?" said Mama Bear. "Baby Bear never said anything to me about inviting Goldilocks."

"Kids, they're always up to something," said the woman. "Which is why it's best if you and I talk rather than the fathers."

"Talk about what."

The woman shifted in her seat, or rather Papa Bear's chair.

"Goldilocks was wrong to come into the house when you weren't home, but she was invited."

The woman paused and Mama Bear felt like telling the woman it was time for her to go, but instead, she sat waiting patiently because now the woman was about to tell her the real reason for her visit.

"My husband is quite upset over the way your husband growled at Goldilocks, and he wants to press charges."

Mama Bear felt her fur bristle, but the woman quickly added, "But I told him he was over-reacting. I suggested that I come here and talk to you. If you tell the police not to press charges for trespassing, then my husband won't press charges for terrorizing a child."

Mama Bear took a deep breath and then, showing great restraint, thanked the woman for bringing the cakes and said that she would contact the police herself. That seemed to settle things, and the woman had wasted no time in leaving.

Left alone in her kitchen, Mama Bear finished the washing up.

In their house, all the chairs were the same. What a ridiculous idea! She might as well have said that males and females were the same. And her husband helped with the housework. Surely that was not the natural order of things, but on the other hand, if Papa Bear knew what was involved in keeping a house just so, would he take more care? And the idea of earning money? Goldilocks' mother had hit on something Mama Bear didn't like to think about. Her aunt Grumblebear's husband had died in a hunting accident, leaving the she-bear to raise 3 baby bears on her own. But surely Papa Bear had made provisions for them if he was injured or worse, killed. Suddenly, the security she relied on felt not quite 'just so'.

That's why she let loose with her string of expletives. The world that had been just so this morning was now turned inside out. Goldilocks broke in, but she'd also been invited. Papa Bear was right to be angry, but he'd over-reacted. And who was stuck cleaning up the mess? What was even more irritating was that she enjoyed having a visitor, and not just because she brought cakes. They hadn't agreed on everything, but they'd found some common ground, and the woman was right; they were better suited to resolving hostilities than their husbands.

At the sound of the door, Mama Bear set the timer and placed the roast in the oven. Baby Bear's feet padded down the hallway, and Mama Bear felt a warm glow spread through her furry chest.

"How was school today?"

"We're having class elections tomorrow, so I have to make a campaign poster."

"And who are you campaigning for?"

"For Goldilocks and me."

"What!", exclaimed Mama Bear. "The girl who ate your porridge, broke your chair and fell asleep in your bed?"

"She apologised Mama and asked if I would be her running mate. She says we can win because we're in the majority. There's 15 females in our class and only 12 males."

Mama Bear sat down in her chair. What was this world coming to? Bears and girls being friends. Females running for president. What was next? Baby Bear saying she wanted a career? How was she going to explain this to Papa Bear?

Chapter 10

VERNA

"I'm confused," said Flo. "I mean, I get that Baby Bear is a girl and I've been sort of conditioned to think of him, I mean her, as a boy but I thought you said this was a story about a hussy."

"It is," said Ginger, "but words, as Margret pointed out, are like our preconceived notions about whether a woman should be a stay-at-home mom or a dedicated professional. They are subject to change."

"So, are you changing the meaning of hussy?" Asked Flo.

"No," said Beatrice. "I think Ginger is telling us that the meaning of the word has changed over time."

Ginger smiled. "Like spinster, hussy has a long and interesting history."

Beatrice laughed. "If anyone made the connection, it should have been I. Housewife in my day referred to what Flo might call a sewing kit."

Then, turning to Margret, who'd paused her knitting, said, "And

Margret should have picked up on that too because even the first Oxford Dictionary defined housewife as a small pouch for sewing tools."

"We didn't use the Oxford Dictionary," replied Margret. "We used Websters."

"But I still don't get the hussy connection," said Flo as she searched in her pocket for her phone.

"Partly its due to English spelling being a bit ad-hoc before dictionaries became the definitive source for what words meant and how they should be spelled," said Ginger. "So housewife could be written as huswif, huswyfe, hussive, hussif, or hussy."

"Got it," said Flo, who'd been typing on her phone. "According to Google, it was actually the word housewife, or some variation thereof, that took on its negative connotation. And it also says that a housewife could -"

"That negative meaning had disappeared by my time," said Margret.

"That's true for the word housewife," said Ginger, "but the word hussy retained the connotation of a 'loose' woman."

"The meanings diverged," said Margret, "but the implication that women fell into one of two categories, a woman who a man looked after or one who looked after many men, remained."

Verna, who'd been quietly sipping her wine and didn't seem to be interested in the origin of words, said, "No one uses the term housewife anymore. It sounds too fiftyish, no offence Ginger. We came up with the word homemaker. Far less sexist." She took another sip and muttered, "The personal is political."

Flo repeated the words, then said, "I'm not sure I understand."

"It was a slogan from my era. It means women getting stuck with all the domestic duties, getting paid less, and, I might add, being beaten in the home, the whole male supremacy thing, is indicative of a political structure that needs to be changed. While some of the more radical feminists wanted to abolish any differences based on genitalia, more moderate feminists just wanted men to treat us as equals." She sighed and took a long drink. "We failed on all counts."

"That's not true," said Flo. "There was the Equal Credit Act that allowed women to have credit cards."

"Great, now we can rack up debt."

"And the Pregnancy Discrimination Act."

"Which doesn't ensure that women won't be overlooked for promotions."

"The outlawing of marital rape."

Verna merely looked up but didn't say anything.

"The Equal Employment Opportunity Act."

"And how well is that working for you?"

"Well, how about no-fault divorce."

"You're right," said Verna. "That was a win"

"I think what Verna is pointing out," said Beatrice, "is that you can legislate equality, but someone will always find a way around it."

"And laws are subject to change," pointed out Ginger. "What changes hiring practices is not laws but necessity. Before WW2 in the U.S., there was a marriage bar on women, but after the war, that practically disappeared because we needed teachers, while in other countries where men needed jobs like in teaching, the marriage bar remained in place. It's necessity - not votes - that creates change."

Margret, listening to the exchange, started to speak but then decided to let the dialogue continue between the modern-day women. Verna, however, decided to join in.

"I thought that the postwar years were a step back," she said, "and I didn't want to go backwards. I wanted more than just a job. I wanted a career. I wanted the same opportunities that my male counterparts had. But I also wanted a home and family. Men could have both, so why couldn't I?"

"Because someone has to take care of the children," said Ginger, "even with day care, someone has to drop off them off and pick them up. Someone has to stay home with them when they're sick."

"A lot of men do that now," said Flo, but Verna didn't seem to be listening.

"I couldn't keep up with it. If I focused on my family, the men at work said I wasn't as dedicated as they were. They said that's why I didn't get promoted like them. Huh! I worked twice as hard, and I was every bit as good."

"Maybe the problem was that men still saw the home and kids as belonging to the woman. It's different now."

"Is it?" said Verna. "Chloe believed she could have it all, a career, a family. She said there was no need for feminism. That it was outdated. Yesterday's news. Well, where did it get her? In the 50s, women were told to make themselves attractive when their husbands came home because 'there were girls in the office' and 'men will always be men' but by the 80s we were sold the idea that we could 'bring home the bacon, fry it up in a pan, and never let him forget he's a man.' In other words, we exchanged housewife for superwoman."

Verna stopped, exhausted from her outburst.

Outside, the rain had turned to snow, and the wind, while still blowing, made less noise. The fire crackled, and Margret turned another row.

"I wanted life to be different for Chloe. I wanted to protect her from the guilt of feeling inadequate at home and feeling that she always had to be better than everyone at work, but mostly I wanted to protect her from harm."

"Chloe knows that," said Flo.

"How do you know that?" said Verna.

"Because Chloe and I are closer than you think. She told me how she wanted to be like you but not you. Or maybe like a better version of you. Someone who could find some sort of balance between home-life and work. Something between the personal and the political."

"Maybe you should tell that to her partner. He thinks she's responsible for his being laid off. Somehow, it's her responsibility that men no longer have a role in society. That somehow, because she doesn't need him, that he has the right to beat her."

"I'm not justifying his actions," said Flo, "but I think he's frustrated because women have moved ahead and now, he doesn't know what his role is anymore."

"So, we're supposed to understand when men take their frustrations out on the women?"

"I didn't say that, or at least, I didn't mean that."

"Whether you do or don't mean it doesn't matter. What matters is that the courts let him get away with a few slaps. They told him to stay away from her, but did they stop him before he put her in a coma?"

Flo leaned over towards Verna, but Verna pulled away.

"The problem is that men fear women." Margret's needles worked steadily away. "Their first experience of love is in the mother's womb. That's their first and only memory of ever feeling secure and safe. Which makes birth their first betrayal, and I doubt many men get over that, especially since life is a series of betrayals. The mother weans her child, sends him to school. He falls in love, but it doesn't last. He marries, goes to work. Has children. They love their mother and fear their father. He's always yearning to return to that last safe place, but he can't."

The needles clicked and no one spoke.

Then Verna leaned forward, "That's a pile of bullshit, Margret." She slouched back in her chair. "And besides, if there were any truth in it, then why don't women resent their mothers?"

"Who said they don't?" said Margret. "They just show it in different ways." She held up the piece, adjusted it slightly, turned it around and started another row. "Besides, every girl has the potential to be a mother. There's a certain solace in that."

"That's a very old-fashioned view," said Flo. "Some men are very maternal and some women aren't."

"Women have wombs; men don't."

"And is that your definition of what makes someone female?" asked

Flo. "Because if it is, then every woman who has a hysterectomy has just had a sex change."

The evening was turning fractious, and Beatrice wasn't sure if it was because of the hour or too much wine or that change that she felt in the air, but regardless of the source, she thought it might be best to call it a night.

"Perhaps we'll postpone Verna and Flo's stories for another time. It will be light in an hour, and the storm seems to have died down—"

"I want to tell my story."

Verna's statement shocked Beatrice with its uncompromising tone. She looked over at Margret who continued knitting as if nothing had changed. Ginger shrugged her shoulders as if to say, 'Why not' and Flo said, "If you feel you're up to it, then I think you should."

Beatrice leaned back and said, "Then we're agreed, Verna, please begin."

Verna drained her tankard, and as she filled it up again, she spoke.

"What little girl doesn't dream of becoming a princess? For that, I blame the fairy tales we women tell our children. But I suppose it's only natural for a little girl to want to live in a beautiful castle with a handsome prince who adores her and gives her everything her heart desires. And for what? Because she is beautiful and innocent? How long does that last? We hesitate to tell them about the dangers, instead filling their heads with notions of romance and everlasting love. It's no surprise, then, that when that little girl outgrows the pink tulle and fake tiaras, she continues to long for that happy ever after life. She longs to walk down the aisle, all eyes upon her, dressed as a princess in virginal white. But that's where the fairy tale ends. The prince, it turns out, isn't always charming, and the 3-bedroom castle with its fireplace and tidy cottage garden is actually owned by some landlord or banker and the only fairy godmothers are the gossips who come to welcome the next unwanted baby. And so the happily ever after turns into a monotony of days that follow each other in shocking similarity until at last the children are grown and gone and the fairy-tale princess has time to herself. She looks in the mirror, and what does she see? The princess sees not herself, but in her place an aging queen who is both envious and frightened of all the women who are younger and more beautiful."

Verna paused to look around the group.

"And if an older woman seeks to save a younger one from making the same mistakes, she's labelled an old hag, a witch or a crone."

She turned to Flo. "When I'm finished, you can look up the history of all those terms, gossip, hag, witch, crone, but for now we'll accept their current meaning." She took a long gulp from the tankard and then, setting it on the floor, she stared into the fire. Shadows flickered across her face as she said, "I call my tale The Girl In The Tower."

Chapter 11

THE GIRL IN THE TOWER

To live your entire life in a tower gives you a different perspective from those who live at ground level. Down there, you're surrounded by the hubbub of all that noise and clutter while, up here, there's little to distract the mind from contemplation. I used to think that's why my guardian, Frau Gothel, placed me here. After all, she often said that I was above the common riffraff. That she'd seen something special in me, even as a baby. What that special something was, she never said. And although I was raised in isolation, Frau Gothel made sure I received an education. She taught me to read and brought me books, but what I only learned recently is that books, like people, vary in quality. Some, while well written and richly bound, have no substance, while others, although poorly expressed and of moderate print quality, are rich in thought. And then there are those that purport to speak the truth but actually subvert it. They are the dangerous ones. And it turns out; they are also the most seductive.

But I'm jumping ahead of myself. I should explain my relationship to Frau Gothel. As far back as I can remember, she was the one who cared and looked after me. I can't remember how I came to understand that she was not my mother. Perhaps I had called her that, and she corrected me, but somehow, I came to the realisation that I had missing parents and I became obsessed with knowing what had happened to them.

At first, Frau Gothel said that I was too young to understand, but that didn't stop my questions. I was persistent. Over and over, I begged her to tell me about them until one day she lost her temper and, grabbing me firmly by the shoulders, knelt in front of me. Her eyes flashed with an intensity I'd never seen before. Her voice, harsh and full of vitriol, frightened me more than the words she spat in my direction. The gist of it was that my mother was a foolish woman and if I wasn't careful, then I too would grow up to be weak and foolish. It was my mother's foolish requests, she said, and my father's even more foolish acquiescence to her demands that landed them on the wrong side of the law. Although she never said as much, it was obvious that my parents had done something unforgivable and that it was only because of her, Frau Gothel, that I was spared the same fate as them. Then, loosening her grip on me, she swept out of the room, taking my dinner with her.

The next day, she took me from her house to this tower. It was only here, she said, that I would be able to avoid the evils and temptations of the world. And for my part, I promised that I would be an obedient child if only she would not abandon me. That's when she took me by the hand and pulled me over to the window. I thought she was going to push me out, but instead, she pointed at the ground and said, "Look at all those common folk below. See how small and insignificant they are. This tower is not your punishment. Far from it. I've brought you here to protect you because the world is cruel, especially for a young, innocent girl, such as you. You're too young now to understand, but in time, boys will begin to notice you. They will tell you pretty lies and covet what is yours. And once they take what you have to offer, they will leave you. I know this because once I was young and vulnerable. You may feel sad or even angry because your parents traded you for their own foolish desires, but there are worse things that could have happened to you.

The world, she explained was a frightening place, especially for young women.

"It's better to be protected by this tower at least until you are old enough to protect yourself."

"And then will I be freed?"

"Women can never be truly free as long as men see us as objects." Then she sighed. "But we can learn how to keep ourselves safe."

In those early days in the tower, I thought Frau Gothel might teach me how to defend myself, but instead she brought me books and told me stories that reinforced how dangerous the world was. In that way, I came to understand that the tower was my sanctuary. There, I was both safe and comfortable. Still, I suffered from loneliness, so one day Frau Gothel brought me a bird. It was bright blue, and it came in a lovely cage with a swing, and Frau Gothel made me promise to give it fresh food and water daily. She also warned me to keep the cage door shut. From morning to night, while I stared down at the world below, my little bird sat on its swing and sang. In my innocence, I thought the caged bird's song was meant for me, but then one day another bird appeared. It sang the same tune and hopped close to the cage. How wonderful, I thought, imagining the wild bird wanted to join mine, so I opened the cage door. To my horror, instead of the wild bird hopping in, my tame bird hopped out. Then, before I realised what was happening, they both disappeared out the window.

When I told Frau Gothel, I expected her to scold me, but instead she said that my little bird had taught me an important lesson.

"Your bird had everything provided to it, but it didn't appreciate how good it had it."

So you think it will come back if I leave the cage door open?"

"I doubt that very much," she said.

"But why not?" I asked. "It was always happy, sitting on its perch and singing. Surely once night comes, my bird will get cold and hungry and think to come home."

"Silly child. By now, a cat has probably caught it or perhaps a hawk. The world outside is dangerous; it's a lesson that too many learn the hard way."

At first, I thought there must be some truth in Frau Gothel's words, that my bird had made a mistake leaving its comfortable home. Then, several months later, I spotted two blue dots flitting through the trees. I thought it couldn't be them, but then I heard them sing. I always thought my caged bird sang because it was happy, but seeing it in the wild, I understood why my caged bird really sang, and that's why I threw the cage out the window.

Life went on. Frau Gothel brought me more books to read. She taught me to play the flute. Even gave me a telescope so I could observe the stars. My knowledge and understanding of the outside world were growing, but it wasn't only my mind that was expanding. I was used to my body getting bigger. Frau Gothel measured my height on the wall. She weighed me on the scale. But these changes were different. My body wasn't just getting bigger; it was changing, morphing into something I didn't understand. With no mirrors in which to see myself, I turned my telescope from the heavens to the village. There I observed what Frau Gothel called the riffraff. Children chasing each other. Not in anger but with a kind of joy. I saw the older boys and girls pairing up, and I thought of my bird and its counterpart. I observed how the older boys would grab one of the older girl's hands and they would slip into the woods only to return smiling sometime later. I noticed that once they were in public view; they parted ways, pretending not to notice each other. I did not understand this behaviour, but I dare not ask Frau Gothel either. Instead, I searched the books she gave me, but they only talked of equations and theories. They couldn't explain why people acted one way in public and another in private. Nor could they explain why my chest began to swell and hair appeared in places it had never grown before. I found myself staring at this new body, wondering what evil was at work, and then one day Frau Gother arrived to find me cowering under the covers. My nightclothes were covered in blood, and I had come to the conclusion that because I used my telescope to spy on others instead of turning it towards the heavens, I was being punished. I thought I was dying.

Frau Gothel cursed, but I think it was more to herself than me.

"I should have warned you," she said as she cleaned me up and showed me what to do when my monthly, as she called it, arrived. "Remember how the caterpillar hides inside its chrysalis and emerges as a butterfly."

I nodded, wondering if I was about to sprout wings.

"Well, humans also change. You are changing from a girl into a woman."

As she explained about the changes, she combed my hair. It had become quite long, so she'd taken to braiding it.

"Womanhood is like this braid. It is both beautiful and cumbersome because you must learn to care for it. You must keep it clean and orderly. And yes, with each passing year, it becomes more of a burden, but at the same time, you will learn to live with it."

After that, she brought me new items of clothing to restrict those parts of me that were changing, but there was nothing she could do to constrain my mind. I continued to watch the people in the village and found myself concentrating on the young men. I imagined the best-looking ones smiling at me the way they smiled at the young women, and I wondered what went on the wood that made them both happy and shy.

It was about this time that Frau Gothel measured the length of my braid. It was quite long, and she no longer combed its entirety. Instead, she only braided the ends as they got long enough. It had grown faster than my body. In fact, by the time I was fifteen, it lay coiled up like a golden snake in the centre of the room. On the day Frau Gothel came to measure my braid, she said that there was a rumour in the village about a beautiful girl who lived in a tower. She asked if I spent much time in the window. I thought she had discovered my secret spying on the village, but it was the reverse that concerned her.

"This is a most dangerous time for you because men want most what they think they can't have. For that reason, I'm sealing up the entrance."

"But Frau Gothel, how will I live?"

"Don't worry, child. I will still visit every day, but instead of using the stairs, I will call up to you, and you will drop your braid so I can climb up."

What makes Homo Sapiens so successful is their ability to adapt. I read that in one of my books, and I found it to be true. Frau Gothel and I adapted to the new arrangement. I would see her heading towards the tower, checking to make sure she wasn't being followed and then she would call out, "Rapunzel, let down your hair," and I would drop my long gold braid and feel the weight of her as she climbed its long length. Otherwise, little changed. By day I trained my telescope on the village, and by night I turned it back towards the night sky.

Similarly, Frau Gothel always came to visit when the sun was in the sky, so you can imagine my surprise when I heard her call out late one night. I had been staring up at the stars, so hadn't noticed her coming, and, of course, it was too dark to see her from my perch at the top of the tower. It certainly hadn't occurred to me that someone else knew our secret. My first hint that all was not as it should be was when I felt that first tug on my braid.

It didn't feel like Frau Gothel, but by the time I realised something was amiss, it was too late. I backed up as the stranger clambered over the windowsill. I was standing in my usual spot with the kitchen table behind me, and my fingers sought out the knife I kept there as the stranger revealed himself. He was tall and lean with dark hair that was pulled back from his face and held in place by a ribbon. I recognised him as one of the villagers. A particularly popular one with the girls, as I'd seen him slipping into the word with several of the prettiest girls. Seeing him close up, I began to see why. Even in the moonlight, dull as it was, I could see the sparkle in his blue eyes. Nor did the lack of light from my candlelit room diminish the smile he turned on me.

"I haven't come to hurt you."

There was that look about him, the one I'd seen boys and girls in the village exchange, and his voice was gentle as if speaking to a scared animal, which indeed I was.

"Forgive me, I was drawn here by your beauty."

I liked the sound of his words, but he had entered my tower without my permission, so I kept my hand on the knife.

He took a step in my direction.

"All you have to do is say the word and I will leave."

In my head, I heard Frau Gothel's voice telling me to say "go," but there was another voice, a more insistent one that said, "Tell me your name."

He blushed. Despite keeping his head bent ever so slightly downward, like a submissive dog, I could see the blood rush up his neck and flood his cheeks. It made him look less threatening.

"My parents named me after a singer they liked."

"And who was this singer?"

"They named me Prince."

He took another step forward, and I whipped out the knife.

"I swear it's my name."

"And what do you want, Prince?"

I said his name with the same sarcasm that I imagined Frau Gothel might use.

"I only wanted to see you in person and perhaps to talk to you."

Frau Gothel had warned me that talk could be as dangerous as actions, but I was curious. Even more than curious, I was attracted to this person so unlike myself. I told him to sit, and he obliged, taking my chair by the window while I continued to stand, my knife at the ready. I asked him about his family and his life in the village. He replied that his family was well-off. They owned a large piece of land, and their house was second only to the castle. The more he talked, the more relaxed I became. The knife remained in my hand, but it no longer interested me. I told him about my books and my telescope. He said that I was the first girl he'd met who was interested in science and math. For some reason, that pleased me. Then the sky began to lighten, and I said that he needed to go before my guardian found him here.

"Perhaps I can come back," he said as he climbed over the windowsill. "I could bring you some other books, ones that aren't so serious. More about human nature than science," he said. Then added, "That's if you're interested."

And that was how it started. He became a regular visitor and, as promised; he brought books, and, as he said, they weren't like the ones Frau Gothel brought me. The books he brought talked of love but not in the same way as the philosophers in Frau Gothel's books. Similarly, Prince's books described sex, not as a mechanism of reproduction but as desire. His books aroused more than my curiosity, and I asked Prince to explain this thing called lust.

Frau Gothel used language to explain things to me, but Prince was more about show than tell. He came quite close and placed his hand on my chin and brought his lips close to my ear. I thought he was going to tell me a secret, so I stood quite still. But it wasn't my ear his lips touched. It was my neck. That touch, as light and gentle as a summer breeze, sent a tingle through my body. My stomach dropped the way it did when I looked at the ground from my great height. Then, his arm moved around my waist and drew my body next to his. I felt like chocolate left in the sun. His lips moved from my neck to my cheek but found a home on my own. As he pulled away, I thought I might collapse. In that moment, everything fell into place. This is what went on between young couples in the wood, and I understood why they looked both happy and shy. I allowed my fingers to explore first the muscles of his back, then up his neck until they lost themselves in the hairs on his head as I pulled his lips back towards mine. The ribbon holding his hair dropped to the floor, and I remember thinking how lucky he was not to be weighed down by a long, thick braid such as mine.

I have no idea how long or how many ways we explored each other's body, but I remember waking to the song of birds and the delicious warmth of sunlight. At first, I stretched luxuriously as if waking from a beautiful dream, but then I felt his body in bed next to me. In terror, I shook him awake. He opened his eyes and quickly jumped up. Grabbing his clothes, he threw them on, not bothering to button his shirt and without so much as a word of goodbye disappeared out the window. In fact, my braid was still hanging down when I felt Frau Gothel pulling herself up. She was halfway up and asking why I had let down my braid before waiting for her call when I noticed the ribbon on the floor. There was no time to pick it up so as she clambered through the window, I stepped back to hide it with my feet, even as I explained, "Frau Gothel, I was at the window when I saw you coming so I thought I'd have your ladder ready for you."

She set down her basket and looked around the room as if seeing it for the first time.

"There's something different this morning. The room smells different."

"Oh, I think it's those flowers you brought me the other day. I forgot to change the water, and they started to smell musty. I threw them out, but I think the odour lingers still."

"And you, Rapunzel. You look different this morning. Are you well? You look feverish."

"You may be right," I replied. "But I'm sure it's nothing that a little more sleep won't cure."

"In that case, I won't stay long. I've brought you some fresh fruit and biscuits."

Turning away to unpack her basket, I reached down and picked up the ribbon, wadding it up in my fist. She turned back. "Are you sure I shouldn't stay and look after you?"

I assured her it was nothing more than a summer cold or perhaps the coming of my monthly curse, which sometimes forced me to stay in bed.

"Give me your hand."

Reluctantly, I held out my empty hand, and she held onto my wrist. I thought at any minute that she was going to ask what I was hiding in my other hand, but instead she said, "Your pulse is a little fast, which can be caused by fever." Again, she suggested she stay, and I suggested she go, but after much back and forth she at last agreed to leave. Once she was gone, I wound my braid back into its coil in the middle of the room and fell into my bed, vowing never again to let Prince into my room. It was a promise I had every intention of keeping even as I tucked the ribbon under my pillow.

Promises are never made with the intention of breaking them, and yet that is what happens. Frau Gothel often said that the road to perdition was paved with the best of intentions. For all my studying of the great writings, I confess that I'm not sure that my intentions were ever good, never mind the best. The reality was that as soon as I heard Prince whisper my name; I dropped my braid and we were soon engaged in the sort of activity that Frau Gothel had warned me against. My days were spent discussing grand thoughts with Frau Gothel and nightly indulging in lascivious acts with Prince. It was no wonder Frau Gothel remarked one day that I looked worn out.

"Are you sleeping well?"

I replied that my monthly curse was unusually painful, so Frau Gothel said that some girls suffered more than others and promised to bring me something. The truth, however, was the exact opposite. It had been several months since I'd had any bleeding, but I was not schooled in the ways of women, so I was not alarmed.

"At least you're not losing weight," she said the next day when she brought me some peppermint to ease my pains. "In fact, I think we may have to let out that bodice and perhaps even this skirt."

As her hands ran over my abdomen, they stopped. Her face took on a serious demeanour, as if she was listening to a noise that was barely audible. I'd seen dogs do that. Perk up their ears at some noise beyond what the human ear can detect. A dark shadow crept across her face, and I felt suddenly exposed. I prepared myself for Frau Gothel's verbal assault, but this time she took me by surprise. The slap, so quick, so violent, knocked me to the floor, but even that didn't assuage her anger. Like a hound pouncing on a rabbit, she was on me, pulling me to my feet.

"Who is he? Who has done this to you?"

I tried to protest, but it was useless. I told Frau Gothel that it was Prince and that we were in love.

"Love? What do you know of love?" She paced around the room. "Do you know why you're called Rapunzel?"

I shook my head.

"Your mother told your father she craved rapunzel, a kind of weed that only grew in my garden. Instead of asking me if he could have some, he crept into my garden at night and took what was mine. I caught him, but instead of punishing him for trespassing, I allowed him to have all the rapunzel he desired, but in return I wanted the child his wife was carrying.

My face must have betrayed my confusion, so Frau Gothel spelled it out.

"Your father traded you to fulfill his wife's desire. The baby belonged to the mother just as the rapunzel belonged to me. He had no right to either, but men believe they are entitled to take what they like from a woman because they think they have all the power."

"No, it's not like that between Prince and I."

"Isn't it? If you're so sure, let me put him to the test. When he comes, I want you to behave as if everything is normal. Drop your braid and let him come up here and face me."

I should have known. They call that hindsight bias, but in this case, I think I really did know. It's that consciously, I chose not to see it, so when I heard him call my name, instead of saying "run", I said, "come". I felt his weight pull on my braid, and the knife was there on the table. At any time,

I could have cut him loose, but no, I let him climb. You might think I envisioned him telling Frau Gothel that he loved me and that he was planning to take me away from my tower. That he would make me his wife and look after me and our child — but even then, I think I knew what he would say. In the books he brought me, they spoke of happily ever afters, but planted in my brain were Frau Gothel's words about my foolish parents and how they'd abandoned me. Whether Prince foolishly stood by me or selfishly abandoned me, the end was always going to be the same.

He clambered over the window, a look of eager desire that rapidly changed to horror as Frau Gothel stepped out from behind me. At the same moment, a cloud must have passed in front of the moon, for the room darkened. Something unspoken passed between Frau Gothel and Prince.

"I know you," she said. "I know you and your family."

"And I know you. My father told me all about you. He said there were women who begged to be used by men, so to deny them that right was its own kind of sin."

"Your father didn't ask. He took just as you've taken."

I could see how the muscles in Prince's body tightened while Frau Gothel's body, in contrast, became more fluid.

"You're no different from your father. You defiled my innocent girl."

"I never made her do anything against her will."

"That's what you said about the miller's daughter."

"The miller's daughter? She had every boy in the village before she had me."

"And the girl sent to clean the cinders from your parent's mansion."

"She enjoyed it."

"And the girl you found sleeping in the wood. Did she enjoy it?"

"It was her own fault, making herself vulnerable like that."

"And Rapunzel? Did she make herself vulnerable?"

He glanced in my direction and then returned to Frau Gothel, who was edging closer and closer.

"I only meant to teach her, which is more than I can say for you."

"And then what?"

"What do you mean, then what?"

"She's with child, so now I want to know what you plan to do about that?"

"I don't plan to do anything. I never said we'd live happily ever after. I'm a Prince and she's—"

"I'm a what?"

Up until now, I'd remained silent while these two talked about me as if I were some object. Frau Gothel talking as if I belonged to her and could be locked away like some precious ornament, and Prince talking about me as if I were some insignificant plaything, and all the while the baby in my belly was calling out for my attention.

"I told you," said Prince. "You're a beautiful woman, and I've never been able to walk away from beauty. It's not manly."

Before I could respond, Frau Gothel replied in her own way. The air around her crackled as if charged with static electricity. An aura blacker than ink swirled around her. I'd seen her anger and rage before, but this time it was off the scale. Prince, wasting no time, threw himself over the windowsill, and I stumbled forward with the unexpected tugging on my braid as he scrambled down, and then I saw the flash. It was too quick for me to register. The knife fell, slicing my braid as if it were butter. Prince's scream lasted longer, and then Frau Gothel was leaning out the window and laughing. I exploded, and before either of us knew what was happening, she was tumbling herself.

I don't know if I sat for an hour or a day or maybe even a week. I know that I cried nonstop and that my tears watered the thorns that grew near the base of the tower. They grew up the wall and reached my perch in the sky, and it's on the topmost thorn that a little blue bird came and sat. It sang, and somewhere deep inside the girl in my womb replied with her own song. It was her song that roused me. It was her future that gave me the strength to climb through the thorns and brambles until at last I reached the ground.

They say the tower still stands, although now it's almost hidden. They say the word hag means witch, but I've read the books Frau Gothel gave me, and I know that the word hag is actually a reference to the word hedge. It wasn't sorcery or witchcraft that Frau Gothel practiced. She thought the tower would protect me, but I've since learned that until the world becomes a safer place for females, all girls need to learn how to protect themselves both emotionally and physically. I think Frau Gothel would agree when I say every girl needs to have a bit of hag in her.

Chapter 12

FLORENCE

*V*ERNA FINISHED SPEAKING. THE WIND AND SNOW HAD STOPPED. The fire had almost gone out, and Margret's needles sat idle in her lap. No one wanted to be the first to break the silence, and so they sat as the sky, now devoid of clouds, shifted from black to grey, erasing all the stars but one. The shadows, without light to inspire them, had withdrawn, and the cozy feeling of a warm fire inside while the storm raged outdoors and given way to a greyness that was neither cold nor warm. What had last night's winds destroyed? Beatrice looked out at the garden and the trees beyond. There the moon hung, snagged on the topmost branches as if it were fighting to get through them. Its pale light gave the snow a bluish hue, like that of a body that no longer contained life- drained of that essence that some called a soul. She shivered while somewhere far away, a cock crowed

Florence spoke.

"I was sorry to hear about your daughter."

Verna looked in Flo's direction, but her eyes were distant. A moment passed, and Flo wondered if Verna had heard her. Then Verna shifted and, staring at the tankard in her hand, said, "The doctors are hopeful."

Raising the tankard, she drained what remained, then said, "Which is more than I can say for the courts."

"Oh, Verna, that must have been so hard," said Ginger.

Verna shook her head and shrugged her shoulders. A movement so slight it might have gone unnoticed except that everyone in the circle was focused on her every move.

"You know what she said the time before?" Verna looked from one concerned face to another. "She made excuses for him. I told her to leave, but she refused, and now this." Another pause. "He'll get away with it. They always do."

No one spoke. What could they say? What happened to Verna's daughter was nothing new. Every one of them had experienced such violence themselves or knew someone who had.

"Perhaps we should call it a night," said Margret. "Florence can save her story for next time. You don't mind, do you, Flo?"

"Of course not," replied Florence, but as she stood, Verna grabbed her arm and said, "Absolutely not. Remember our vow. We will not be silenced."

Flo sat back down.

"We will not be silenced," she whispered, and the others repeated the same.

Verna sighed, the hint of a smile played on her lips as her eyes closed. Then her head dropped, and the tankard slipped from her hand. It clanked and rolled across the slate floor, resting as it hit Flo's foot. There was a general looking around as each woman sought to judge for herself if they should stay or go.

"Should we take her home?" asked Ginger.

"Let her sleep it off in the chair," said Flo.

"In that case," said Beatrice, "why not tell your tale, Flo?"

"Perhaps now is not the time."

"Flo, you've welcomed us into your house. You've listened attentively to each of us, and now it's our turn to listen and learn.

Florence picked up the poker and shuffled the remaining logs until at last a little flame shot up.

"I bought this house because of this fireplace. I don't use it all the time. There's a modern heat pump that adjusts the temperature with the touch of a button, but I thought the fireplace was more appropriate for our gathering. Each fall, I choose a few fallen branches to chop up and stack for the future. You can't use green wood for a fire. It doesn't burn well. And some wood, like pine, burns too fast, and its resin turns into creosote when burned. It sticks to the chimney and becomes a fire hazard. That's why I stick to hardwoods. When I use my heat pump, I don't think much about the fuel it burns."

She paused to look at each of the other women.

"Don't get me wrong. I worry about using up the Earth's resources. I'm as concerned about the effects of fossil fuels on the climate as anyone, but when I build a fire, there's a direct connection between what I do and what I get in return.

She placed the poker back in its stand and sat back. The fire that moments before had appeared to be going out, had renewed life. Flames danced around, creating shadows that danced on the walls and the ceiling.

"A lot of people think you throw some logs in the hearth, maybe some newspaper and then light it with a match, but to get a fire going takes planning. You build it in layers. It doesn't matter if you build it top-down or bottom-up, but certain elements are necessary. You need something highly combustible, leaves, twigs, paper. I like diversity in my top layer, so I use all three. You need smaller logs that will burn up first to create a layer of ash, and then you have the big logs that burn for a long time.

I've listened to your stories, and I'm reminded of how far we've come, not only as women but as humans. Some of my generation worry that the future is bleak, but I don't think it has to be. I think humans have always adapted, but they adapt best when they work together. There's an old story about the father who calls his sons together. He gives them a bundle of sticks bound together.

Margret nodded and said, "He asks the sons to break the sticks."

"Which they can't," said Ginger.

"Until the father undoes the bundle and breaks each stick."

It's a well-known story because, simple as it is, it's so true. Common sense really, but common sense isn't as common as we might think. Even within this group, there are those sticks that haven't been bundled up with the others, and that makes them more vulnerable. My story is about a girl who wears a red cape, but she could be wearing anything; jeans, a sari, a *byrqa*. In fact, she doesn't have to be female. They could be someone whose genitalia dictate one course while they would run another. Their skin could be brown, yellow, white or green for that matter. None of these things are relevant. What matters is that we can't see them. Not because they're invisible. We don't see them because they are not part of our bundle of sticks. They're the ones that lay scattered on the ground where they can be stepped on and easily broken. If they go missing, who will notice? I'm hesitant to tell this tale because it is an indictment of our movement as much as it is about society.

Florence waited.

"You heard Verna," said Margret. "We should not be silenced, not by the world or those who would rule, and certainly not by us. I for one, would like to hear your tale."

The others nodded their agreement. So as the knitting needles resumed their clicking and with the first light crept in, Florence settled back in her chair, began, "My tale is a short one and like Verna's all too common."

Chapter 13

MISSING AND PRESUMED

THIS IS THE STORY OF A MISSING GIRL. THE SORT YOU NEVER hear about because she wasn't a princess. She wasn't the brightest and fairest in the land. She wasn't pretty or popular, and she didn't have suitors vying for her hand. She wasn't one of those girls you could say had a bright future because girls like her didn't have bright futures. She was likely to wind up like her mother and her mother's mother before her, poor, pregnant and likely unwed. She was one of those girls who were so indistinguishable from each other that they became invisible, which is why no one notices when they go missing. And if they were reported missing, they weren't listed as missing. They were listed as runaways because it was common knowledge that girls like that ran from abuse or poverty. Or they ran away with boys who pimped them in the back streets of town. They were sold, traded, discarded. There were so many ways for a girl like that to disappear. For girls like that were of no consequence. That's what everyone thought when she went missing, so it was not surprising that the authorities were slow to act. What was surprising was that the coroner held an inquest which is the only reason her story has been recorded. The following is a transcript of that inquest.

Coroner's Inquest ATU 333 Cautionary Tale

The proceedings started with the mother's testimony. She said that the day the girl went missing was a normal day, a bit foggy in the morning but by noon the skies had cleared and the afternoon, while brisk, was sunny. It was because of this coolness that the mother told her daughter to take her cloak. The Coroner asked the mother to describe the cloak.

"It's the red cloak commonly worn by schoolgirls, your honour. It has a hood and, for some reason, is called a riding cloak, but only rich girls have horses."

The Coroner asked the mother to tell him about that morning.

The mother explained that there was to be a fete at school, so she'd baked biscuits for the girl to share with the other students. And, as there were extras, gave the girl a basket of them to drop off at her grandmother's on the way.

Postscript *: Later, the investigators would state that it was the unusual circumstances — the biscuits, the school fete, the drop-off at granny's — that delayed their search. It certainly wasn't because the girl was ordinary. They had followed standard procedures. Nothing more. Nothing less. This was obvious in the Sargeant's testimony.*

Coroner: Why did it take so long to begin the search?

Sargeant: Your honour, the mother reported the girl missing on a Friday afternoon. She was hysterical as people like her can get.

Coroner: People like her?

Sargeant: Single mothers living on the fringes. There's always dramas in that area, but most of them get sorted without police intervention.

Coroner: Continue.

Sargeant: At the time, the mother stated that the girl hadn't returned home at the normal time. We asked the usual questions. How old was the girl? Had the mother checked with the girl's friends? Was the girl unhappy?

Coroner: And what did she tell you?

Sargeant: As I said, your honour, she was quite hysterical, so it was difficult to get the story straight.

(Sargeant checks his notebook)

I calmed the woman down. Offered her a cup of tea. She declined. She told me the girl was fourteen. I suggested that girls of that age were unpredictable, rebellious even. The woman replied that her daughter was a good girl- that she always came straight home after school. I asked the mother if she worked, and she said yes. She did laundry. I asked the mother if her work meant that she wasn't always home when the girl returned from school. This angered the mother, and again I had to calm her down. I said that if she wasn't home every day, how did she know that the girl always came straight home. I pointed out that girls that age often lost track of time. They got distracted picking flowers or talking to their girlfriends. The mother said she'd already checked with all the girl's friends, and they hadn't seen her all day.

Coroner: So, is this when you learned that she hadn't shown up for school?

Sargeant: No, your honour. That was not apparent from what the woman said. She never said that the girl didn't show up at school; she only said the girl's friends hadn't seen her that day. How was I to know that that meant the girl never showed up for school?

Coroner: I understand. Please continue.

Sargeant: I suggested to the mother that perhaps the girl had friends the mother didn't know about. Friends of the opposite sex. The mother said that she and the girl were close, but I took that with a grain of salt.

Coroner: And why was that Sargeant?

Sargeant: We've all been there, your honour. At the risk of being indiscreet, I had experiences I never told my parents about.

Coroner: Alright, Sargeant. Moving on.

Sargeant: At this point, we had another call, some business about a cat and a fiddle disturbing the peace, so I told the mother that she should go home and wait. The girl would no doubt show up in due course.

Coroner: No mention of the basket of cookies or the trip to granny's?

Sargeant: Not at that time, your honour.

Mother: I tried to tell him. He wouldn't listen. Kept cutting me off.

Gavel knocking

Coroner: Silence in the courtroom. Madam, You'll get your turn. Now, Sargeant what happened next?

Sargeant: Well, we retrieved the fiddle.

Laughter

Coroner: Silence! Sargeant, I was referring to the girl.

Sargeant: Oh, that. Well, the mother came back the next day and said she'd gone to granny's house to look for the girl but that the old woman's house was empty.

Coroner: So, is this the first you knew of the girl visiting grandmother's house to deliver biscuits?

Sargeant: It wasn't clear at this moment, no, your honour. The mother only said that she'd gone to the grandmother's house to see if the girl was there. She didn't say that the girl was going there on her way to school, and there was no mention of biscuits.

Coroner: And you never thought to ask?

Sargeant: We were still assuming the girl had run off, your honour, and that she'd turn up eventually.

Coroner: So, at this point there was no suspicion of foul play?

Sargeant: Not at that time, your honour. The mother only said that she went to the old lady's house and found it empty.

Coroner: And you didn't find that strange?

Sargeant: I asked if the old lady might have gone for a walk, and the mother said that the old woman wasn't well enough to go on a walk. That's when I asked if the girl might have stopped by her grandmother's, and the mother said, of course. That's why she went there in the first place.

Coroner: So, at this point did you visit the grandmother's house?

Sargeant: Not right away. You see, it occurred to me that the girl had likely gone to the grandmother's house and, finding the woman ill, had taken her to hospital.

Coroner: So, did you check the hospitals?

Sargeant: Not at that time, your honour. You see, we had a more pressing matter. A farmer reported his prized cow was missing, possibly stolen. I suggested the mother go to the hospital and make her own enquiries while we went in search of the missing cow.

Coroner: Then what happened?

Sargeant: Well, we found that the cow had jumped over the moon, which explained how she wound up in the neighbouring farmer's field.

Mother: I told him the house was ransacked.

Gavel banging.

Coroner: One more outburst like that, Madam, and I'll have you removed. Now, Sargeant, can you stick to the case at hand?

Sargeant: Apologies, your honour, but you see, it proves my case. Girls, especially teenaged ones that go missing, aren't so different from cows. They usually turn up in someone else's field. They come home eventually, and we had no reason to believe there was any misadventure.

Coroner: So, is it common to not attend to missing person reports for two days?

Sargeant: Not quite. If we suspect foul play, we begin immediately, but in the case of teenagers like the girl in question, we take a more cautious approach.

Mother: She was a child. A vulnerable child, and you did nothing.

Coroner: I have repeatedly warned you, Madam. Bailiff, remove the woman.

Coroner: So, at what point did you begin your investigation?

Sargeant: On the Monday, your honour.

Coroner: Let me get this straight. The girl went missing on the Friday, but you didn't get involved until the Monday?

Sargeant: Well, you see, your honour, the mother came back on the Sunday and said she'd checked the hospitals and even contacted the girl's father. I asked why she hadn't contacted him earlier, and she said that they weren't on the best of terms. That she had a restraining order out on him. Now, that changed things a bit. It was starting to look like a domestic case, so I contacted the local social worker and asked him to check on the father as we had real police work to attend. A silver spoon had gone missing, so I told the woman to go home and wait for us to get back in touch.

Coroner: And how did that turn out?

Sargeant: Open and shut case. It turns out the dish ran away with the spoon. We apprehended both and—

Coroner: The girl, Sargeant. Had the father seen the girl?

Sargeant: Sorry. I mean, no, your honour. The social worker said that the father hadn't seen the girl. Turns out, the girl and her father were estranged because she didn't like her stepmother.

Coroner: So now it's Monday morning. Is that when you attended the grandmother's residence?

Sargeant: Not first thing, your honour. There was a sighting of a wolf near the schoolyard, so we went there first. Turns out the boy who spotted the wolf was playing tricks. Anyway, while we were there, we interviewed the teacher and learned that the girl hadn't shown up for school on the Friday.

Coroner: And was it common for the girl to skip school?

Sargeant: According the schoolteacher, the girl had missed some days, saying that she had to look after her granny.

Coroner: And so you were still labouring under the assumption that the girl was alive and well.

Sargeant: That's correct, your honour. Before we assembled a search party and put up notices, we decided to interview the grandmother.

Coroner: Which I presume you did on the Monday.

Sargeant: We were going to your honour, but we had a report of two children who claimed they were incarcerated by an evil witch. We had to organise for them to be returned to their father, so it wasn't until Tuesday that we went to the grandmother's house.

Coroner: And what did you discover?

Sargeant: The first thing we noticed was that the place was a mess. The bed was unmade, furniture was toppled, and there were cookie crumbs everywhere.

Coroner: At this point did you suspect foul play?

Sargeant: Not at this point, your honour. You know how it is with old people. They get slack when it comes to keeping things tidy. But what did catch our attention was the basket. It was green and yellow. Quite similar to one that had been lost by a lovely young lady in the village. She said she dropped it on her way to market, so we decided to check with her to see if she recognised it.

Coroner: Didn't it occur to you that the basket was the one the missing girl was carrying when she left home?

Sargeant: It was such a fine basket, your honour, that we thought it was too good for the girl in question. Unless of course she'd found it. That's why we took the basket in question to the lady who'd lost hers. She said that no, it wasn't hers but did offer us a cup of tea. They're a fine upstanding family, so we could hardly refuse.

Coroner: But having ascertained that the basket didn't belong to this fine, upstanding lady, I presume you went to the missing girl's house.

Sargeant: It was quite late at this point, your honour, but we did go first thing the next morning.

Coroner: And did the mother recognise the basket?

Sargeant: She did your honour.

Coroner: And at this point, did you organise a search party?

Sargeant: Well, we were discussing doing just that when a woodsman arrived. He said he'd discovered a wolf's den that contained some bones. We had him take us to the spot. There was no wolf, but as he said, there were bones and – other items.

Coroner: Can you describe these – other items?

Sargeant: We found a bloody nightie and a piece of red cloth.

Coroner: And on seeing these items, what did you do?

Sargeant: We asked the mother to identify them, and she recognised the nightie as belonging to her mother.

Coroner: And the piece of cloth.

Sargeant: She also recognised it as belonging to her daughter's cloak.

Coroner: And what of the wolf? Was the animal found?

Sargeant: Yes, your honour. We had a report of another missing child. It was the boy from the school who was known for playing pranks. If I told you his name, I'm sure you'd recognise it because his family has a large sheep farm outside town. That's why, despite his pranks, we immediately sent out a search party. A local woodsman managed to track down and cornered the wolf.

Coroner: In the same den?

Sargeant: No, it was on the other side of the wood, but we believe it was the same wolf. It has been destroyed, your honour.

Coroner: Well, I think that we have enough evidence to conclude that the girl and her grandmother were killed by the wolf and that the wolf has been despatched. Based on your testimony, I think we can close this case. You may step down, Sargeant.

Postscript: *Not long after the Coroner's findings, the mother disappeared. No one noticed because they were busy mourning the loss of the boy who everyone said had a bright future and would be greatly missed. The whole case of the missing girl and her grandmother might have been forgotten if another girl hadn't disappeared walking through those same woods. This time it was a lovely girl from a solid family, and this time the police began their search immediately. They found the girl alive. She'd been abducted by the woodsman and hidden in his hut deep in the woods. When they searched his house, they found a torn red riding hood. The kind schoolgirls wore but of course by then everyone had forgotten the girl and so the story remained that she and her grandmother were eaten by a wolf.*

Chapter 14

As One Tale Ends So Another

THE MOON, HAVING FOUGHT HER WAY THROUGH THE TREES OF the wildwood, paused briefly to gaze upon the alterations made by the storm, then she left, taking the last of the night with her. In its place remained a cloudless blue sky and a world coated in pristine white. It was a blank canvas waiting for the artist's first brushstroke, a marble stone waiting for the sculptor to reveal the object within, a blank page eager to capture the writer's thoughts. Beneath the snow, however, nothing had changed. The plants in the garden had not been swept away, nor had they lost their colour. One of the tall trees had toppled, but it wasn't gone. It had simply changed its perspective. The snow would melt, and most things would go back to the way they were, but Beatrice knew this storm was only the first. More would come, and they would be stronger and more devastating. Last night's storm was an announcement that the change that was in the air yesterday had arrived.

She looked at her hands, folded neatly in her lap. That fresh flush of life she'd felt on seeing her sisters again had ebbed away, and her skin was once again paper thin, the flesh barely covering bone. Yesterday, that had frightened her - this business of fading away - but in this early morning light, she understood, and understanding brought with it acceptance.

"I'm sorry, everyone," said Flo. "I was so involved in telling my story that I'm afraid I let the fire die."

"I don't think we need it anymore," said Ginger, standing up to stretch. Twisting her shoulders, first one way, then the other, she glimpsed the garden and gasped. "We've had the first snowfall, and it's not even autumn!"

Margaret looked up from her knitting. She expressed surprise. "The first snowfall is always magical, isn't it?" Then with a sigh, she added, "But it won't last long once the sun gets to it." She shoved the remaining skein and her needles into her bag and asked, "Can someone give me a hand up?"

Both Ginger and Flo rushed to help her to her feet, and as she stood, the piece she'd worked on during the night toppled to the floor.

"I'll get it," said Flo, reaching down to pick it up, and as she held it out for Margret to take, she said. "The colours are beautiful. Is it finished?"

Margret, who was busy arranging her skirt and straightening her sash, replied. "It's not the sort of piece that is ever finished, but for now it's yours, and next time I'll teach you how to knit, if you like."

"I would love that," said Flo as she placed it around her shoulders. "Do these colours signify anything special, like the blue on your sash?"

"Indeed, they do. Every story told last night is encoded in the pattern and the colours."

"Like the knitters who kept track of troop movements?" asked Ginger.

"Yes, like that." Margret, who was occupied gathering up her bag and picking up her tankard from the floor. "You can study it while you decide what theme we'll have for our next gathering."

"That's right, Flo. It's your turn but can you please pick something brighter?" said Ginger. "Fairy tales are so dark."

Flo was still studying the scarf. "But, Margret, how can I read it if I don't understand the code?"

"Don't worry; like wisdom, that comes with time. Now do I have everything?"

"I'll get your coat," said Flo, "but won't you stay and have a cup of coffee or tea before you go?"

"I wish I could, but there's a meeting of the Society of Former Delegates of the Seneca Convention, and if I don't get some sleep beforehand, I shall fall asleep during the reading of the minutes."

"Sounds incredibly exciting," said Ginger, looking over at Flo and exchanging a smile.

"Oh, and I'll be sure to ask them about the Hauden, whatever tribe. I found that most interesting, Flo," added Margret, oblivious to their exchange. "Oh, and for your theme, can you choose something where women show off their political prowess?"

"I'll see what I can do," said Flo, handing Margret her coat. "And what about you, Ginger? Can I get you something?"

"I'm afraid I have to go as well. The McCutcheon woman is expecting twins, and they could come at any time." Picking up the box with the two remaining tarts, she said, "We all know that baby's chose their own birthday but when there's twins, there's likely to be a squabble, especially if one's a girl and the other's a boy. Then, there's no telling when they'll be born or even if they'll be born on the same day." Holding out the box, she added, "Now, Flo, I'll leave these last tarts with you."

"Are you sure you don't want to take them home?"

"There's plenty at home, and besides, Verna may want one when she wakes up."

They looked over at Verna, who snored and twisted around in her chair. The three women standing over her laughed, then Margret said, "I have someone picking me up; shall I take Verna home?"

Flo shook her head. "Let her sleep. In the end, it's the only medicine that heals the soul."

"That and time," said Ginger.

"Healing is a gift from the gods," added Margret.

All the chatter around her chair woke the sleeping woman and, opening her eyes, she mumbled, "Have I missed anything?"

"Just Flo's story, but maybe she'll tell it to you over coffee and a tart," said Ginger.

Verna sat up lazily and looked out the window. "What time is it?" Then, looking at her phone, she sat up.

"What is it?" asked Flo as Verna grabbed her shoes.

"Sorry, Flo, I've got to get to the hospital. Chloe's out of her coma and asking for me." She wriggled and tugged on her skirt as she said, "Let me know what you've decided on for a theme, but can it please be something that shows how women succeed?" She bent down to put on her shoe, then having second thoughts about wearing them, stood back up.

"Even when the odds are against them," added Margret, lifting Verna's sweater back onto her shoulder.

"I'll have to let you ladies know when I come up with something," said Flo as she pulled Verna's coat from the closet.

"Ladies," humphed Margret.

"How would you have her refer to us?" asked Ginger. "As girls?"

Flo held Verna's coat for her to slip it on.

"I'll have you know," said Verna, searching for her car keys, that at one time, the word girl referred to an adolescent of either sex.

Ginger held up the box of tarts and Verna selected one, saying, "Isn't it interesting that to call a grown male a boy is demeaning but to refer to a female, even ones as old as us, as girls, is perfectly acceptable."

"Perhaps crones would be more appropriate."

They all turned to face Beatrice.

"That's a bit harsh," said Margret, sounding offended.

"Not at all," said Beatrice, lifting herself out of her chair. "There are some who think the word crone comes from the French word *carogne*, which means carrion. But there is another source for the word, one that's often overlooked - and that's corona. Maid, woman, crone; these are the phases of a woman's life, and we should be proud of them. Patriarchal men would have us believe that once we are no longer able to bear children - for them - then we have no further function. But crones can be wise women, as well as fearsome witches and withered hags."

"No offence, Beatrice, but crone still sounds old and ugly to me," said Verna, dangling her keys in triumph.

"Then what would you call us?" asked Margret.

"I rather like domestic goddess," said Ginger.

Verna raised an eyebrow.." And on that note, I think I'll get going," And with shoes in hand, she shoved the tart in her mouth and headed for the door, but as she opened it she exclaimed, "Flo, there's snow on the ground!"

"Take my boots; they're by the door," said Flo.

"You're a godsend," said Verna.

Flo waved her off and turned back to get the other's coats when she stopped.

"That's it."

"That's what," said Magret.

"Our next theme," said Flo, "I think it should be goddesses."

And with that, the evening officially came to a close. Margret and Ginger took their leave, thanking their hostess, leaving only Beatrice. Flo found her standing by the big window looking out at the garden with its orchard leading up to the wildwood beyond.

"Would you like a cup of something?"

Beatrice ignored Flo's question. Instead, she said, "I'm sure I'm not alone when I say that i wish Chloe had been here tonight to tell her own tale. For now, she has her own battles to fight, but I believe once she is fully recovered, she will join us again. But tonight, Flo, it's your stories and your insights that gave me hope for the future. You opened my eyes to the need to find value in each and every person. Feminism, in the past, has been about empowering women so they can find their place in a patriarchal world; one in which the strongest succeeds and all others fail. But women are powerful in other ways. Margret's princess who says take me as I am or I'll find someone who does. Ginger's Mama Bear who clings stubbornly to her family traditions but accepts that her daughter may choose a different path, and Verna's girl in the tower who courageously risks death to escape through the hedge of thorns to seek an uncertain future, and even my own spinster who leaves behind a castle to live the life of her choosing. All these women show their strength by standing up to the pressure of those who would make them accept less than they deserve. You, on the other hand, talk about- I think the word is inclusion - although I might use the word respect. Whatever word we attach to it, it means valuing others. Your tale reminded me that the world won't be safe for any of us as long as the most vulnerable among us is ignored."

She wrapped her arm around Flo's waist and pointed at the sky. Already the sun was melting the ice on the trees, but on the horizon, there was a dark line.

"When I came here yesterday, there was a strong wind that pummelled me. I wasn't sure what it portended, for the winds of change are unpredictable, and I admit it frightened me. More storms are coming, and they will be worse than last night's. Men may conquer other men, but they can't conquer nature. To survive, humans will need to band together. It will take all the knowledge, skill and determination to weather the storms that are coming, and that means finding solutions, even in the least likely places. Now, it's time for me to go as well. Can you bring me my cloak?"

Flo thought about Beatrice's warning as she pulled the heavy cloak out of the hall closet. The message was frightening, and she wasn't sure if she, or indeed, any of them, was up to the task. She wanted to know about this great change that Beatrice mentioned, but as she returned to the living room, she found it empty. She called out the elder's name, but there was no response.

$$\textit{The Angels Series}$$

Book One When All Hope Is Lost

When did history become her story. According to the Old One's version of events, the pandemic of 2029, called the Desolation, didn't bring about the change even though it killed all adult males. Nor was it the way the pandemic changed the male genome so that they never survived their twentieth birthday. The real change was brought about by Evelyn Perkins, the Saviour of the Greater Republic of Melbourne. But who was she really saving?

Book Two Pray To The Dead

By the year 2049, it's women who rule a world where men no longer grow old. Everyone is on the run but there are fewer and fewer places to hide. As the government closes in on the Subversives, the fugitives find friends in strange places.

Book Three For Where There Are Harps

As the Old One reveals more and more of the Republic's intent to eliminate males, the girl is both enthralled and worried. Even now, 20 years after the Great Upheaval, these allegations are treasonous.

Visit Fiction+Speculation

For more short stories and speculation

visit

<u>https://www.alyceelmore.com/</u>

www.ingramcontent.com/pod-product-compliance
Lightning Source LLC
Chambersburg PA
CBHW070503170726
48291CB00008B/2639